SAM CRESCENT AND STACEY ESPINO

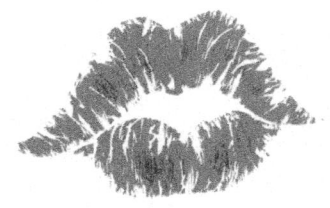

EVERNIGHT PUBLISHING ®

www.evernightpublishing.com

THE BIKER'S DIRTY LITTLE SECRET

Copyright© 2022

Sam Crescent and Stacey Espino

Editor: Audrey Bobak

Cover Artist: Jay Aheer

ISBN: 978-0-3695-0506-4

ALL RIGHTS RESERVED

WARNING: The unauthorized reproduction or distribution of this copyrighted work is illegal. No part of this book may be used or reproduced electronically or in print without written permission, except in the case of brief quotations embodied in reviews.

This is a work of fiction. All names, characters, and places are fictitious. Any resemblance to actual events, locales, organizations, or persons, living or dead, is entirely coincidental.

SAM CRESCENT AND STACEY ESPINO

THE BIKER'S DIRTY LITTLE SECRET

Straight to Hell MC, 2

Sam Crescent and Stacey Espino

Copyright © 2022

Chapter One

Heat radiated off the asphalt, the late afternoon sun unrelenting for the fourth day in a row. Brick craved to take his Harley out for a long ride, to feel the cool breeze against his heated flesh. But no, he'd be taking the pick-up truck with no AC into town. Lord's old lady wanted to start raising laying hens at the club, so he'd been assigned to get all the materials to build a coop. This was definitely the last thing he wanted to be doing today, but no one refused an order from the prez. He wasn't sure why Lord hadn't asked one of the prospects to do this shit. As VP of the Straight to Hell MC, he had better things to do with his time.

He pulled the whiny door closed after climbing up into the driver's seat. The building center was just on the outskirts of town, supplying lumber and other essentials to the area. He rolled down the windows, but even the air felt stale at these temperatures.

The drive was uneventful. He couldn't complain about much these days. There hadn't been any club drama for months, and he hoped it would continue. He was still getting used to Ally being a permanent member of the club. The prez's old lady made Lord a father. Things were changing. Brick wasn't sure how he felt about it.

He missed the days when he'd run into hellfire by Lord's side. Now his prez was taking the cautious approach because he had a family to think about, not just the club. Women made men weak—there was no way around that fact.

The building center finally came into view up the road. Brick was sweating through his t-shirt and felt like shit. He couldn't wait to get back to the club and take a long, cold shower.

He parked in front of the main building and hopped out of the truck. Brick always wore his cut, but in weather like this, he'd gladly break his own rules. He tossed his cut on the passenger seat and tugged off his t-shirt, using it to wipe his brow.

Brick grabbed the list Ally had given him and headed into the building. After entering the lobby, he closed his eyes for a moment and just breathed. The AC felt like fucking heaven.

"Hot out there?"

He opened his eyes. A girl behind the counter stared at him.

"I can handle hot," he said. "Whatever's going on outside is next level."

She giggled in response, a sweet feminine sound. He noticed her gaze roving down his body. He immediately patted himself down in response, feeling for

THE BIKER'S DIRTY LITTLE SECRET

an exposed weapon, but realized it was just because he was shirtless.

He was used to the club whores chasing after him, but this girl looked nothing like them.

"It's terrible. I don't have AC at home, so I've actually looked forward to coming into work this week. And trust me, that says a lot," she said.

He stepped closer, leaning against the counter. People didn't usually talk to him, especially local women. He was used to being feared. The chitchat was somehow refreshing. There was something about this chick and her classic girl-next-door looks that pulled down his walls. She wore her hair in a thick ponytail. It had to be a good two feet long.

Brick shook his thoughts away.

"Sorry, I'm rambling. How can I help you?"

"I don't mind," he said. "What's your name, anyway?"

She pointed to the badge on her shirt.

He ran a hand down his face. "See, the heat is really getting to me. Nice to meet you, *Callie*."

She bit her bottom lip, and it was sexy as fuck.

"I don't think I've seen you around before. Do you live close by?"

"Not too far," he said.

It was at that moment he realized she didn't know he belonged to an MC. In her eyes, he was just another civilian. And he had no desire to fill her in on the truth.

She leaned over the counter on her elbows and slipped him a card. He glanced at it briefly but was more entranced by the intensity of her blue eyes. She even smelled sweet, a subtle vanilla.

"Don't tell anyone in the yard, but it's a family discount. You may as well get some use out of it."

He took the offering. "No family?"

She shrugged. "Just me, but the boss doesn't need to know that."

"Thank you, Callie."

After a cleansing breath, she grabbed a notepad. "Let me get your order before I keep you here all day."

Honestly, he didn't mind. For the first time in a long time, he felt human. Back at the club, he was feared, idolized, sometimes hated. And he was dangerous. Addicted to violence.

He slipped her Ally's list.

"A chicken coop? I'd love to have chickens, but I think my apartment complex would frown upon that." She winked.

"I guess so," he said. "Hey, if we're successful, I'll be sure to bring you some fresh eggs."

"We? Are you married?"

"No, no woman. I was talking about my brothers."

"A big family sounds fun." She spoke while punching codes into her computer.

He didn't answer. No sense creating a web of lies when he could keep his mouth shut instead.

Another staff member came in from the back, glancing over at him. Brick raised his chin, an unspoken challenge. He was always ready for a fight. But the guy only set a stack of purchase orders down beside Callie.

"Thanks, Jeff."

"You okay in here?" he asked. Brick wanted to tell him to fuck off.

"Actually, this is a pretty big order. Can you get a new skid of 2x4s down with the forklift?"

"Yeah. Sure." He left the way he came, looking over his shoulder at Brick one more time before closing the door. Did he recognize him as a biker? Would he tell Callie?

And when did he start giving a shit about what other people thought?

"I think I have everything on your list." She handed him back the paper from Ally. "If you pull your truck around back, the boys will load you up as soon as they pull down that wood."

"Thanks for your help."

"My pleasure," she said.

He shoved the list into the pocket of his jeans and left the building center. The entire time he waited around back, he kept thinking about the things he *should have* done and *should have* said to Callie. It was all he could think about. He barely focused on his surroundings until there was a knock on the side of his truck.

Brick jerked in his seat. He hadn't even noticed the guy inches from his face.

"You're all loaded," said one of the yard hands.

"Thanks."

He started up the truck and began to ride out of the building lot. Brick had gotten what he came for, and now he could head home. This was what he wanted—short and sweet. Only he couldn't pull out onto the road. Instead, he did a hard right turn, bringing him back to the front office.

For a good five minutes, he sat there in the truck, trying to convince himself to forget about this town girl and move on with his life. She was nobody. He had no time for socializing outside of the club, and never had any desire to do so. Relationships with outsiders were frowned upon. Besides, once a girl like Callie knew exactly what he was, she'd run the other way and never look back.

I'm a fucking idiot.

Brick went back inside the building center. Callie was at a desk behind the counter. When she saw him enter, she got up and approached the front.

"Was the order all right?"

"Everything was fine," he said.

Why did he suddenly feel like he was twelve years old, his mouth dry, and nerves on fire? He was completely out of character, and the guys at the club would laugh their asses off if they could see him now.

"Did you want to order something else?"

He ground his teeth together, his jaw clenched. "What time do you get off work?"

"Five. Why?"

"I wanted to thank you for your help. Maybe take you out to dinner or something."

She remained quiet, and he regretted opening his mouth in the first place.

"Or not," he said. "It was just an idea."

"No, I'd love to go to dinner."

He nodded. "I better drop this shit off and get ready then. I'll pick you up at five."

****

Callie was still in a state of shock after the hot guy left. And she hadn't even asked for his name. It was difficult to think straight when he wasn't wearing a shirt. His body was golden and ripped like a gladiator. The ink on his arms was unlike anything she'd ever seen. She probably should have refused his offer. He was a classic bad boy, she had no doubt about it. But he didn't act like an asshole, and for some reason, she felt comfortable around him when she was normally quite shy around men.

It was difficult to focus on work for the rest of the afternoon. None of the men in the yard had shoulders and biceps like her guy. When they'd talked to each other, she'd had to remind herself to make eye contact and not keep checking him out. She liked everything about him,

THE BIKER'S DIRTY LITTLE SECRET

from the gruff tone of his voice to his impossibly dark eyes.

What would he think of the real her?

He'd only seen her from behind the counter. Once he saw her fat ass, he'd probably regret asking her out. She wiped her sweaty palms on her jeans. He was picking her up in a couple of hours, right after work, so she'd have no time to fix herself up. In an ideal situation, she'd take a shower and change into something pretty.

Jeff came in and sat at his desk. "Any new orders?"

"A few online. No more walk-ins."

"That guy give you any trouble?" Jeff asked. "He looked like trouble."

"He's just a chicken farmer. Relax."

She didn't want any more questions and didn't like her mystery man being judged.

"A farmer covered in ink?"

She shrugged.

Honestly, Callie didn't want to dig deeper. She just wanted to enjoy the moment. He'd asked her out on a date, so she was still on cloud nine.

She'd been so focused on working and surviving that she had little time to worry about herself, her love life, or her future.

So many thoughts crowded her head. What would happen when he dropped her off? She didn't want him to see the shithole where she lived. Or what if he wasn't what he seemed to be at all and he ended up dumping her body in a ditch somewhere?

The minutes ticked on until only ten minutes remained until her shift ended.

Her heart raced. What if he didn't even show up? What if he did?

Callie shut down her station and gathered up her

belongings.

She used the staff bathroom to fix herself up. After pulling the elastic from her ponytail, she ran her fingers through her hair the best she could. When she looked beyond the glass, she still couldn't see the white pick-up truck in the yard. Her heart sank. She didn't realize how much she'd wanted this to work out.

Callie usually walked a mile to the town, then took the bus to her apartment at the far east end. One day, she'd have enough saved up for a little car, but until then, it was a tedious routine that wasn't optional. And much worse in this heat.

She began her trek through the dusty yard, checking her watch again. Maybe she should wait a few more minutes in case he was just late. Her life was so full of disappointments that she doubted he'd show up. It had only been about five months since her grandmother passed away. That pain was still fresh. She'd raised Callie alone, giving her some semblance of normalcy in her childhood years. Her parents and cousins were all messed up on hard drugs, stealing and conning people to support their habit. Her grandmother tried to shield her from the worst of it, but they were mostly MIA, and she wasn't so naïve.

Her mother showed up out of nowhere to claim her grandmother's trailer after the funeral, effectively leaving Callie homeless for a couple of weeks until she got her current bachelor apartment. They hadn't spoken since.

The roar of a motorcycle made her heart race. She always feared running into a biker on her lonely walk to town. She'd been lucky so far. Callie was well aware there were at least two big clubs in the vicinity. One of them was currently building a new clubhouse, and they came in for supplies frequently. She wasn't allowed to handle those invoices, so she knew something wasn't right about their orders but kept her mouth shut. It wasn't her business.

When the bike slowed down behind her, she began to panic. Why hadn't she invested in some pepper spray? She turned her head to her side when the bike crawled next to her.

It was him ... her mystery man.

He cut the engine and swung his leg off the bike. "Canceling our date?"

She swallowed hard, alternatively glancing at him and then the bike. He looked so different than earlier. Well, he had clothes on for one—a fitted black t-shirt and blue jeans, his hair slightly damp. She wanted to run her fingers along the ink and muscles.

"I didn't think you'd show."

"You've got to give me a chance," he said.

She noticed him less than discreetly looking her up and down. Was he grossed out? She was known for her curves, and often the brunt of jokes around the yard. It was something she was used to but hated nonetheless.

"You ride a motorcycle?"

"You're not afraid to get on back, are you?"

"Oh, you want me to ride on that?"

Callie had never been on a motorcycle. The thought scared her, but she did like the idea of wrapping her arms around his waist.

"It's not so bad. You may even like it." He reached out and ran a section of her hair between his fingers. She was glad she let it down.

"I don't even know your name," she said.

"Brick."

He used a nickname? She wasn't going to complain. It did suit him.

Brick got back on the bike, started it up, then

nodded behind him. She may be twenty-six, but she was still innocent when it came to men. This was all new to her.

She used the excuse to touch him, resting her hand on his shoulder as she straddled the bike. He was hard, and something stirred inside her from the simple touch.

"Hold on tight. These roads aren't friendly."

She slid her arms around him. Her pussy tingled, and it wasn't just from the vibration of the engine. He hit the gas and they were off, the wind whipping through her hair. The breeze felt like heaven, and she closed her eyes, savoring all the new sensations.

Town wasn't far off, so they were soon driving slowly through the streets, finally pulling into one of the strip malls. He parked in front of a restaurant.

"How was it?" he asked once they were both standing on solid ground again.

"Fun and terrifying." She smiled. Growing up in a dysfunctional family made her a good judge of character. Her intuition was usually right, and all the vibes she got from Brick made her feel comfortable.

She tried to pull her t-shirt down farther, to cover her hips. He noticed what she was doing.

"What are you trying to do?"

Callie's cheeks heated. "Cover up? I didn't have time to change."

He shook his head. "Don't try to hide yourself from me. If I didn't like what I saw, I wouldn't have asked you to dinner."

"But—"

"Callie, you have a big, juicy ass. What more could a man want?" He held out his hand and she took it. It felt like the most intimate thing in the world. Brick was completely no holds barred, and she doubted he even

THE BIKER'S DIRTY LITTLE SECRET

realized what he said was inappropriate. She loved that he wasn't trying to play games or put on an act. He was real, confident, and the sexiest man she'd ever met.

They entered the restaurant, and everyone seemed to glance in their direction. Were they that much of an odd couple? Her insecurities got the better of her. Maybe they thought he was too good for her. She bit her lower lip, trying to keep herself together. Dating was new to her, so she had to follow his lead.

Their table was small, near the back of the restaurant with a view of the street.

"Are you hungry?" he asked.

She was starving. Most of the time, she didn't eat lunch. She was on a very tight budget.

Callie shrugged.

He exhaled, a disapproving sound. "Why won't you answer? Are you afraid of me now?"

She shook her head.

"I won't bite."

"Sorry, I'm not used to dating. This is all new to me."

"Well, that makes two of us. Just be yourself. I want to get to know you, Callie."

Silly fairy tale fantasies took over her thoughts. Could he be *the one*?

"Where should we start?" she asked.

The waitress set down two glasses of water, and she noted the way he glared at her. It was only there for a split second, but it sent a warning the waitress heard loud and clear, and she rushed off, leaving them alone.

It turned her on. What was wrong with her?

His presence was so commanding. He made her feel safe and grounded.

Brick took one of her hands, cupping it between both of his. The way he stared at her took her breath away. He was so intense. "Your eyes, they're so fucking beautiful."

She began blushing again. He was rough around the edges, but he sounded completely sincere.

"Thank you," she whispered.

"How old are you?"

"Are guys supposed to ask that?" She felt surprisingly comfortable talking with him.

"I just did."

"Twenty-sex."

He raised an eyebrow.

"Twenty-sex. Sorry. Twenty-six."

Callie wanted the floor to open up and swallow her whole.

"Just a baby," he said, amusement in his eyes. "I shouldn't be here, but I couldn't keep away."

THE BIKER'S DIRTY LITTLE SECRET

Chapter Two

This was the last place Brick should be. Even as he sat opposite Callie, he knew there was nowhere else he wanted to go. Shit was going down at the club, and Lord wanted him there, but he'd used the excuse of needing a night off. The strange look his prez had given him had made him regret the words instantly. He never took time away from the club. He certainly didn't hide his leather cut to impress a woman.

Callie was doing something to him.

Back at the clubhouse, even though everything had calmed down since they'd taken care of Skull Nation MC, they'd been trying to figure out their other problem. Who was the rat within the club? Someone was talking and leaking vital information.

Someone gave the details of where Ally was staying when she'd been attacked at Rancher's farm. She was supposed to be safe from all the shit going down, but somehow, they'd known she was there. There was a leak in the club, and, as VP, he was determined to find it. It was driving Lord crazy not knowing the rat's name. Whoever it was covered their tracks, which again, wasn't good.

They needed to come up with some kind of plan. While the Skull Nation MC rebuilt, Straight to Hell focused on getting stronger.

"I'm a baby. How old does that make you? Not that age means anything. It's just a number."

Callie's smile was so fucking sweet. He loved the way she continually nibbled on her lip. As if she was too nervous to speak. He wanted to take that lip between his finger and thumb and tease it down, but he held himself back.

"You want to know my age?"

"You know mine."

"I'm forty-one."

She paused. "A man with experience."

He smiled and realized it was the first time he'd done so in a long time. "With a great deal I can show you." He reached across the table and placed his hand above hers. He saw the pulse beat even more wildly against her throat. He wanted to kiss her neck. To sink his teeth on her pulse,to hold her against him as he pounded into her tight, hot cunt.

His cock started to harden right then and there, and he had no choice but to look away. He was a grown man, not a child, and here he was acting like a fucking teenager for the woman in front of him. It wasn't like he hadn't had his fair share of club pussy. What sickened him a little was three hours before meeting Callie, his dick had been down the throat of one of the club whores. He didn't know why it bothered him so much, but it did. The night before, he'd been balls deep inside another's ass.

The women came easy to him, and being the VP in the club, they threw themselves at each other and pretty much competed for what they were willing to let him do to them. Looking back now, some of the stuff made him wince, but it had always been consensual. He wasn't the kind of man who enjoyed raping a woman. That shit sickened him. Men who held down a woman who didn't want them, those assholes needed to be fucking slaughtered.

He pulled his hand away from Callie and stared at the menu. The tips of his fingers that had touched her tingled. He was losing his fucking mind over this woman.

"Do you know what's good here?" she asked.

"Can't say. I haven't eaten here in a long time. I'm thinking the steak. It looks good."

"I'll have the house special pasta."

"You sure?"

"Yep. I happen to be addicted to pasta." There she went nibbling her lip and tucking some strands of hair behind her ear.

Again, he wondered what it would be like to wrap the length of hair around his fist with her on her knees, taking her from behind.

Calm down, boy.

His cock was going to come right out of his pants if he wasn't careful.

He nodded for the waiter to come and take his order. The man looked petrified. This was going to cause him a problem. Even though he should tell Callie straight away who he was, he didn't want to. He liked her not judging him. The way she looked at him and not the leather cut. He was a real person to her. Not a trophy or some guy to be afraid of.

Little did she know being with him was bad for her health. Women were targets by rivals. So he had to keep their relationship secret for more reason than one.

"Tell me about yourself, Callie," he said once the waiter had left.

She looked around the restaurant. "There's not much to tell really."

"You've got no family."

"No, not really," she said.

He noticed the way she moved in her seat, seeming uncomfortable.

"Let's not talk about family," he said. "I won't mention mine." He'd already made plans to keep his family life vague, not wanting her to know the truth.

Awkward silence filled the air, and Callie

chuckled. "Is it me or did this seem a lot easier back at work?"

He smiled. She was right. "I'm not used to dating."

"I find that hard to believe," she said.

Brick winked at her. "Because of my charming good looks?"

"You know you've got everything a woman could ever want. There's no reason to seek any compliments." She rolled her eyes, but it was cute. He liked it.

Attention from the whores meant nothing. A simple compliment from Callie meant everything.

"I just don't date." He thought about the club women. There was no reason to. "Not that I haven't been with a lot of women."

"Okay," she said. "That is … an interesting date topic. Tell the woman opposite you how she wouldn't measure up."

"Oh, don't worry about that. You're not like any of the other women."

He noticed her cheeks start to flame.

"Right, of course. I know I wouldn't be."

"Shit, fuck. I didn't mean it like that. You're not like them because I … actually like sitting opposite you." He frowned. "You know, I'm never bad at this with anyone else."

Callie smiled. "This is the first date I've been on."

"And I'm messing it up." He grabbed his water and took long swallows of it, wishing it was something a hell of a lot stronger. "Wait, what?"

"Huh?"

"Your first date?"

She nodded. "I don't date. I don't get asked out. You're the first."

THE BIKER'S DIRTY LITTLE SECRET

"You've had boyfriends, though, in the past, right?"

She started to shake her head then smiled. "My life has been a little complicated."

Brick stared at her. She kept moving the fork around.

"Are you a virgin?" he asked.

Her face went from a nice pale red, to full-on ripe strawberry. What the hell was wrong with him? It was just so surreal to have a real-life good girl having dinner with him. In his world, virgins were as fictional as a fucking unicorn.

"If you raise your voice a little louder, I think the kitchen staff will hear."

Brick glanced around the restaurant and realized he'd raised his voice. Asshole. If the club could see him right now, they'd be taking the piss out of him for fucking months, if not years.

He was the fucking VP, not some normal guy who didn't know his way around torturing a man. This should have been fucking easy.

"I'm sorry," he said. "I mean it when I said I don't date, and you're the first woman I've met that I want to get to know."

"I am?" She tilted her head to the side.

"Yeah, you are. I don't go on dates at all. I don't recall ever taking a woman to dinner."

"Oh," she said. "So, we're both kind of rusty. You just have the experience of what is supposed to happen at the end of a date." She stopped and then raised her hand, shaking it left and right. "Not that I mean this is going to end like that."

"Of course not." He wanted to. He'd love to be the first man to break her in and feel her tight cunt wrapped around his dick as she came. The very thought of it had his cock hardening again, which pissed him off, seeing as he'd just gotten the damn thing under control.

"Tell me what it's like to be a chicken farmer," she said.

"Chicken farmer?"

"That's what you are, right? A farmer. I figured chickens were your thing with what you came in for."

"Right, yes, right." *Shit. Fuck. Shit.* Then he remembered Rancher. "Yeah, it's not something I talk about. There's no reason to talk shop. Let's talk about something else."

"Sure. Sure. So, Brick, is that your real name?" she asked.

"Yeah, it is. Weird parents. What do you like to do outside of work?"

"There's not a whole lot of time to do anything else, but I like to go for walks and I visit the library when I have time. I'm also saving up for some night classes. When my grandmother was alive, she was always upset that she didn't have the money to send me to college. She told me it was a dream of hers to have at least one member of her family do it. Even though she's not with me anymore, I'd like to do it."

"You loved your grandmother?"

She nodded. "Yeah. She was a good woman. A strong, hardworking woman. She believed hard work got you places in this world."

As he looked at her, Brick saw the demons in her eyes. There was something she wasn't telling him. He didn't know exactly what it was, but he intended to find out.

****

The following day, Callie let herself into work, turning on the lights in the office. She moved toward her tiny locker, opened up the combination, and stored her bag inside. Next, she went to the coffee station. Her date with Brick yesterday had lasted long after midnight. They'd been one of two couples left, and it had been amazing. At first, there was awkwardness. There were times she thought he wished to be somewhere else, but that had been her insecurities rearing their ugly faces.

Gradually, they'd started to talk, and she realized Brick was an incredible man. He never went to college, but he was a man of the world. He spoke of traveling and experience out on the open road. The life he'd told her about sounded glorious.

She'd never traveled. Since her grandmother had taken her in, she'd been settled in the trailer until her mother came and took the only home she'd really known away from her. Callie quickly pushed the memories of her mother to the back of her mind. There was no room to think about that woman. She wouldn't allow her back into her life, not that her mother was doing that in the first place. If anything, it was like Callie didn't exist to her mother, and she was more than happy with that.

With the coffee poured, she opened up the rest of the shop as other employees arrived. Jeff was one of the last ones in, and it looked like he'd been partying all night.

He stole the cup from her, and she rolled her eyes.

"You know that's mine," she said, already going to pour herself another one.

"Yeah, and we both know you make much better coffee than me." He took a large gulp and moaned. "See, I feel better already."

She poured another coffee for herself as Jeff fired up his computer. Standing in the doorway so she could see the counter and not be rude to Jeff, she thought about Brick the night before.

The ride on his bike had been ... heady. She'd never imagined it could be fun, but he'd made it so. She smiled, thinking about how it felt between her thighs, but more importantly, how she loved holding on to Brick.

He'd been amazing.

Rock hard.

Since her grandmother died, he was the first person she felt safe with. Like he could protect her from all the dangers in the world. It was a nice feeling.

"You're staring off into space," Jeff said. "You living out one of your fantasies or did you just have pie this morning?"

Jeff was a ... well, she didn't know who he was. One moment, he was nice. The next, he was saying hurtful things. Almost as if she'd done something to piss him off. She never knew which version she was going to get one day to the next.

"Do you think it's going to be a long day today?" she asked, avoiding eye contact.

The end of the date with Brick, that was when he'd been a perfect gentleman. She'd hated telling him where she lived. It was a dump, but he hadn't shown any kind of judgment when she told him. He'd walked her directly to her apartment door and had kissed her goodnight on the cheek. She didn't know for sure if that meant anything. The kiss on the cheek—did it mean he wanted to date her again? Did he hate their date?

She was going out of her mind wondering. This was all so new to her.

It doesn't matter.

If he never came around again, she'd just be happy she got to go on at least one date with him. It was better than nothing. It had been the happiest day she could remember in a long time.

The door to the shop opened, pulling her out of

THE BIKER'S DIRTY LITTLE SECRET

her thoughts. The moment she caught sight of the Skull Nation insignia, she disappeared into the office, giving Jeff the signal.

This was what she'd been told to do. Sitting at her computer, she put on her headset and turned the music volume up to the loudest it could go, blasting her senses.

These were the instructions she'd been given. If she wanted to keep her job, the moment a Skull Nation MC member entered, she was to sit at her computer, complete invoices, and listen to music as loud as she could. She was never to give any of them eye contact.

From her computer station, she could see out of the door.

Just for a quick second, she glanced over the top of her computer. She wished she hadn't. One of the men punched Jeff in the back of the head. He didn't go down to the floor, and she averted her gaze as her heart raced.

"No matter what, you stay behind your computer. You don't watch. You don't even look. If you do, you're out on your fat ass. Got me?"

She'd agreed.

This job was long, but it paid well. She'd been able to save some money up, and she had plans. All of them would come with time and hard work.

Why were they beating on Jeff?

Her stomach twisted into knots. What if one day they turned their attention on her? What would she do? Who would protect her?

When Jeff came in sporting a bloody nose, she removed her headphones. "Are you okay?"

"Fuck, why do you always have to talk? Useless cunt. Get out there and work. I don't pay you to sit around and do fuck all." He was her boss, so she felt helpless and forced to take the verbal abuse.

Getting to her feet, she rushed out of the room. If

she tried to help him or lingered, he'd get more abusive.

Jeff could be an asshole, but he had moments where he was nice as well. He never asked too many questions nor did he demand to know absolutely everything about everyone who worked for him, and she liked that. It made life easy. He didn't judge her, and after a lifetime of being criticized for who she was related to, Jeff was refreshing, even if he was an asshole.

For the entire morning, she stayed out of Jeff's way. Ignoring the tense way the men worked as the Skull Nation stuck around. She heard random shouts but zoned out. By the time it was lunch, she was more than ready to get out of there.

After grabbing her bag, she left the store and headed straight to the small public park area nearby to have lunch. In the height of summer, families and friends would swarm the place, all looking for the perfect shaded spot.

It was hot as fuck, and the park was completely packed. Men and women in different stages of undress were either lying down on the ground or sitting on lawn chairs. There wasn't a spare seat, so she decided not to eat her lunch there.

She walked around until she found a lonely bench. One side had bird shit splattered on it, and the other looked okay. She took her seat and pulled out her bag of sandwiches. Plain old peanut butter. These sandwiches meant she didn't have to splurge on expensive food. Taking a bite, she pretended it was the best sandwich she'd eaten all day.

It wasn't.

In fact, she was sure she was getting sick of peanut butter. She'd been eating the same sandwich for nearly a year and a half.

Yeah, she needed to change it up.

THE BIKER'S DIRTY LITTLE SECRET

Callie was halfway through the second sandwich when she saw *him*. The way the sun shone on him made him look like an angel or something. Brick wore a shirt this time, but it was pulled tight across his chest and arms, which were all heavily muscled, and the ink, damn, he turned her on.

"Hello, princess," he said.

Her entire body lit up like Christmas.

"Hey," she said. Her heart raced as she looked at him. Dropping her half-eaten sandwich to the ground, she stood up.

He bent down and wrinkled his nose. "This is what you call a lunch?"

"Er, yeah, I think so." Why was she tongue-tied right now?

"Nah, it's your lucky day. I'm taking you out to lunch."

"You are?"

"Stopped by your workplace. No one knew where you were. Said you went out to lunch. Figured we could enjoy some food together."

"You always seem intent on feeding me."

He chuckled. "It seems the only time I can get you alone."

He'd stepped closer, or had she imagined that?

Tilting her head back, she looked up at him. She hadn't realized how much taller he was than her. "I'd like to go to lunch with you." She grabbed her bag and stuffed the sandwich inside just in case she needed it later.

She put the strap on her shoulder and held her breath as he offered her a hand.

No hesitation.

She took his hand, and the moment his closed around hers, she felt whole. His grip tightened around hers, and an electrical current zipped up her arm. So wonderful. She tucked some hair behind her ear and ignored the occasional stare.

She didn't care who looked.

Brick had entered her world, and she really hoped this was all real and she wasn't having some kind of cruel dream. As much as she hated to admit it to herself, she'd been hoping for someone to finally see her. Not her past family. Not the poor fat girl. Just to see her, and with Brick, he didn't look through her, nor did he sneer.

He saw her, and it was the headiest thing she'd experienced.

Chapter Three

They'd been dating for weeks. Brick was fucked. All he could think about was Callie. He'd been the perfect gentleman, not even making a move—no kissing, no touching, nothing. He didn't even recognize himself.

She was sweet innocence, and he was addicted.

"Skull Nation are rebuilding," Reaper said.

They'd been in church for the past hour, and Brick was itching to call Callie. Every night, they'd talk for hours, sometimes about nothing at all. She soothed him, made him feel alive for the first time in forever.

"We burned their club to the ground," Lord said. "They're persistent fuckers."

"They have no senior members left," said Brick. "We took them all out. Who the fuck do they think they are?"

"Boss, they're a joke. Nothing to worry about," said Reaper.

"I'm not worried, but I also don't plan to sit back pretending they can't become a real pain in the ass at some point." Lord scrubbed a hand down his face. "Keep eyes and ears open. I want to know when they wipe their fucking asses. Understand?"

Everyone agreed before they started to head out. He checked his watch as he stood up.

"Brick, stay behind," Lord said.

Fuck.

He had a feeling Lord was on to him. His intuition was legendary. Callie was Brick's dirty little secret, a separate life away from the club. He didn't want to tarnish her innocence with the truth of what he really was. It was safer that way, too.

"You find out anything about our rat?" asked

Lord. He stayed seated, but there was something in his eyes.

Brick paced, not wanting to share his secret but also not wanting his prez to think he was betraying the club. The brothers strayed all the time, fucking anything that walked in and out of the club. There weren't any rules that said he could only enjoy club pussy, so why was he so damn nervous?

"Still working on it," he said.

Lord was silent. Brick wanted him to say something, accuse him, anything.

"And the Skull Nation, they're a bunch of pussies. Say the word, and we can finish them off together, like the good old days."

His prez only nodded. Slowly. "Keep an eye out for the rat."

Once Brick was out of the room, he closed his eyes and took a breath. He felt like a traitor and didn't want Lord thinking he was. Brick was one hundred percent loyal to the Straight to Hell MC and always would be. The club was his life.

Anything Lord ordered, he made it happen. He was loyal to a fault, and it helped that Brick was a brutal motherfucker with a complete lack of empathy when it came to rivals.

Once in his room, he crashed on his bed, staring at the ceiling. Was he blind? Pussy whipped? He'd berated so many brothers when it came to women, even judging Lord when he took Ally as his old lady. Women were a weakness, and Brick had always been against the whole idea of love and family.

It was time to take a step back. He rolled to his side and grabbed his cell phone. Callie Johnson had a history, and he'd be a fool to rush in blindly without knowing everything about her. The safety of the club had to come first.

He did some research on his own, then texted Copper to dig up more dirt on the down low. Copper was their in-house hacker, even known for putting the local police department in the dark for forty-eight hours a couple of years back. Within the hour, the techno whizz sent him an email with all the dirt.

Brick was scared to open it, not wanting any of this to end. He actually looked forward to waking up in the morning. Before this affair, there'd been some days he considered putting a bullet in his head.

He scrolled through the email.

Callie wasn't so simple after all. She had a dark past and fucked-up family. The things she had talked about were all the truth—her grandmother's death, her job, the place she lived. He couldn't blame her for leaving out all the messy details.

If she was anything like her family, she sure hid it well. From what he'd come to know of her, she was the exact opposite, and it only made him want to shelter her even more.

He'd keep the information to himself for now. Brick knew some of the characters she was involved with and most were bad news. Sean Rigby, for one, was a notorious loan shark. Why would Callie get hooked up with that piece of shit? She needed Brick in her life to protect her. It would be so easy for a sweet girl like Callie to get soiled by the wrong people—people like him.

The next day, he rode out to the building center. They had lunch together several days a week. He was itching to get more serious with her but kept holding back. Some days he questioned everything about their unorthodox relationship.

He walked over to the picnic bench where Callie

sat. Her big smile lit him up from head to toe.

"Hey, stranger." Brick straddled the bench seat next to her.

"You didn't call yesterday."

He shrugged. "Had a busy night."

She fiddled with her lunch bag, looking over her shoulder on occasion. He didn't like the vibe he was getting from her.

"You okay?" he asked.

"It's nothing. Just some difficult customers. My boss doesn't like me to get involved, but at least I'll get a longer lunch out of it."

Difficult customers? His hackles immediately went up and visions of him gutting the pricks who took out their frustrations on his woman filled his head. He took a cleansing breath.

"You know you don't have to take shit from customers, don't you? It's a job. That doesn't give anyone the right to treat you like garbage."

"I know it's just a job, but it's a job I really need. It's okay, though. They only come around a couple of times a week."

He gritted his teeth to keep from saying anything further.

Brick refocused, tucking some hair behind Callie's ear. The sun picked up the color of her eyes. She was a beauty. When she leaned into his touch, his entire body reacted. He was doing exactly what he claimed he'd never do—falling for a woman. And he hadn't even fucked her yet. He was completely out of character.

"Yo! We're waiting to cash out." Two men walked toward the picnic table. Callie immediately tensed up.

"Is Jeff not in the office?"

"No, nobody's in the fucking office. Are you

going to sit out here on your fat ass or do your damn job?"

Brick stood up, but Callie wrapped a hand around his wrist in an attempt to pull him back down.

"And what the fuck do you want, big boy?" asked one of the men.

Before he could speak, Callie spoke up. "Please, he's just a chicken farmer. We don't want any trouble."

They both laughed.

She attempted to stand up, but Brick set a hand on her shoulder. When she looked up, he shook his head.

"Why don't you prospect pieces of shit back the fuck off?"

They were Skull Nation, and Brick didn't give a shit. As far as he was concerned, they were outnumbered.

The bigger guy lunged forward. "What did you say?"

Within seconds, Brick had him twisted around, a blade against his jugular. The man let out a series of small, measured gasps. "I said, back the fuck off, or I'll have to teach you some manners."

"You don't know who you're messing with, chicken farmer," said the other guy.

"Yeah, I do, a couple of pussies trying to climb their way up an embarrassment of a club." He short punched the guy in the kidney, then shoved him away. After flicking his butterfly knife closed, he rested his hand on the butt of his gun in his jeans with a wink. "Run along."

Once they were out of earshot, he sat back down. Callie hadn't said a word.

"Don't listen to those assholes, Callie." If they weren't in a public place, those two Skull Nation prospects would be dead.

"Brick..."

She was too pale, like she'd seen a damn ghost.

"What's wrong, baby?"

"Those were bikers, Brick. They're dangerous. Oh, my God, this isn't good."

He cooed, cupped one side of her face. "Don't worry, baby girl. Nothing to worry about."

She shook her head. "I don't want anything to happen to you."

No way would he leave until the Skull Nation were gone.

"Eat your lunch, Callie. Nothing's going to happen to me." He leaned closer and kissed her forehead. "I'm invincible, okay?"

"I'm scared."

"What do you know about those guys, anyway?"

"They're Skull Nation and bad news. I'm not even supposed to make eye contact with them."

"Why are they here?"

"Some big project. They've been buying lumber and supplies for weeks."

This was something Lord needed to know about. If the Skull Nation was this far into rebuilding, it was time to tear them down again. He wanted to ask her for specifics, names, locations, but had to remember she knew nothing about his history.

"Keep your distance from them. Any problems, anything at all, you call my cell right away."

"No, Brick."

"Callie, don't argue about this. I'm your boyfriend, and that means I protect you at all costs."

She was silent for a bit.

"Boyfriend?"

A quick flash of insecurity raced through him but vanished just as fast.

"Why do you think I spend so much time with

you, Callie?"

She bit her lower lip, her cheeks turning a soft shade of pink. "It's just that you haven't really tried anything. I didn't want to make any assumptions."

"Should I have tried something by now?"

"I don't know, Brick. I told you, you're my first. I was starting to think you weren't attracted to me and wanted to be friends."

"I'm not looking for friends. I just don't want to scare you away. This whole dating thing is new to me, too," he said.

"You won't scare me away. I've never been happier." She took his hand in hers.

"Just so we're clear, I'm very attracted to you, Callie. Let me pick you up after work. I'll show you exactly how I feel about you."

She nodded. "Okay."

From his peripheral vision, he noted the Skull Nation drive off. This wasn't over though.

****

The rest of the day at work, Callie was nervous as hell. Brick was going to move things to second base, and she wasn't even sure what that meant. She was scared and excited in equal parts.

She couldn't get him out of her mind.

When he'd challenged the Skull Nation bikers, she'd been terrified, but then he'd been so capable. And it turned her on. She wasn't expecting him to be carrying weapons or to know how to wield them so expertly. His strength was impressive. The man was pure muscle and gristle.

He made her feel safe, beautiful, and wanted. She couldn't get enough of his attention.

When she saw his bike pull into the lumber yard, she did a quick peek at the clock. He was right on time, and her heart began to race.

She clocked out and met him out front. He was wearing different clothes, and when he wet his lips, her entire body tingled. He was so rough and sexy. She climbed on behind him as she'd done numerous times, wrapping her arms around his narrow waist.

"Where we going?" she asked.

"Your place."

She didn't have time to argue before he hit the gas, drowning out all sound but the rumble of the Harley. Callie held on tight, loving the feel of the wind in her hair and sense of utter abandon. The destination was what bothered her. It was bad enough when he'd drop her off in front of her apartment, never mind actually coming inside. Her place was a dump, no matter how many little touches she tried to put on the place.

He took a longer way that she didn't recognize, but not before long, they pulled into the lot beside her building. Brick turned off the engine and climbed off, helping her to her feet.

"Maybe we should go to your place," she said.

"Bad idea. This is good."

He took her hand and walked her to the entrance. She cringed as she unlocked the main door. The elevator was perpetually broken, so they took the stairs to the fifth floor. The stairwell stank of urine, making her even more embarrassed.

When she got to her door, she paused before putting the key in the lock. "My place isn't great," she said.

"I'm here for you, not a home inspection." He jutted his chin for her to open up.

Callie swung open the door. Although her place was tidy, it was a bachelorette, tiny and in disrepair. She had a green fridge and a yellow stove. The counter was peeling apart and the laminate floor was deteriorating. Even with the state of her apartment, she could barely afford the rent. She'd had to take some drastic steps when she first started her job since they didn't pay for two weeks.

"Sorry, the landlord doesn't answer calls."

"I like it," he said.

She couldn't help but smile. He walked into the place with no hesitation, exploring everything without a word. Brick picked up a framed picture from an end table.

"It's my grandmother," she said.

"I see the resemblance."

He set it back down carefully. "No other family?" he asked.

"You said we weren't going to talk about family."

"Good memory." He sat down on her brown tweed sofa. "But I think we're past all that now, aren't we? I want to know everything about my woman."

She sat beside him. "Your woman?"

"You're keeping shit from me. Don't hide things from me because you assume I'll judge you—I won't."

Callie swallowed hard. She loved that Brick was no holds barred. There was something irresistible about him, and she couldn't deny him. All she could offer were bits and pieces because no matter how much she wanted to grow closer to him, the shame of her family tree was too much to share.

"My parents are AWOL."

"We have that in common. What happened to yours?"

She fidgeted on the sofa, hating this conversation. "They were addicts. Kids were the last thing they wanted."

"You know where they are now?"

"Brick, I really don't care. I wouldn't want to see them if I could." She shifted in her seat to face him. "Can we please talk about something else? I thought we were moving onto second base."

He raised an eyebrow. "I don't remember saying that."

"Sorry, I'm not thinking straight right now."

He ran the backs of his fingers along her jaw. "No, I like where you're going with this." Brick leaned in closer, brushing his lips across hers. Her heart was going to beat out of her chest. When he kissed her, she closed her eyes. Every move he made was soft and slow like he was dealing with a skittish doe. Her apartment never sounded so quiet. She felt completely inept.

The kiss deepened, his tongue tracing over her lips. The longer they kissed, the more her body relaxed. He pulled her closer, his fingers combing into her hair.

"You drive me crazy, Callie."

He trailed his kisses down her neck. She shivered, resting a hand on his bicep. His lips against her skin had her entire reality spiraling out of control. She opened her mouth to breathe.

"Brick…" The word was breathless and sounded needy even to her own ears.

He returned to her lips, kissing her harder, deeper. She instinctually wrapped her arms around his neck, holding him close. He slid his hand under her shirt, and she tried to suck in her stomach. Brick pressed forward, his big frame enveloping her until she was reclining on the cushion, his rough hand cupping her breast over her bra.

She felt his restraint, but the last thing she wanted was for him to stop. Callie was twenty-six, so it was about time she had a serious boyfriend.

"I should leave," he whispered against her lips.

THE BIKER'S DIRTY LITTLE SECRET

"What? Why?"

Was she too fat? Was he turned off by her? Crazy insecurities kept popping up all over the place.

"I want to be a gentleman. It would be so easy to take everything I want from you, but I won't."

"Do you want to see me again?" she asked.

He leaned back, sitting beside her again. His kind smirk calmed her. "Of course, I do. I'm going to do everything right by you, Callie."

Hand-in-hand, they made their way downstairs. Brick was gaining control of her heart, and she knew he could easily break it.

It was dark outside now, and her neighborhood was unsavory at best. A distant siren wailed and a glass bottle broke out of sight.

When she saw Sean Rigby approach in that stupid black trench coat, she felt a surge of panic. He terrified her, and she didn't want Brick to know all her affairs. She'd been desperate and had no one to turn to for rent money. It had been one of her low points, but she'd had to borrow from the local loan shark to pay her bills. Now the repayment had tripled, and as soon as she saved enough, he'd raise it again. It was a terrifying struggle she expected would never end.

"Callie..."

She held her breath.

"You haven't answered my texts. Be smart. Answer my fucking texts." He walked off without too much drama, and for that, she was thankful. When Brick didn't ask her for information or appear upset like he had early in the day with the bikers, so was surprised.

"Sorry about that," she said.

"No problem. I'll see you soon."

He was suddenly in a rush, backing away, not even waiting to give her the good-bye kiss she craved.

39

As he headed to the parking area, she called out. "Where are you off to?"

"Just tying up a loose end before heading home."

Chapter Four

It would have been so easy to deal with Sean Rigby in the parking lot, but Brick had taken one look at him and knew he needed more information before taking him out. The more he knew about Callie, the more he realized how troubled her life had been. His first assessment of her had been right. She was a total innocent and certainly didn't walk within his world, but due to her parents, she'd been completely swamped, unwillingly, into all of it.

Addicts were trouble. They tended to be selfish, using any means possible to get their next high. Callie's start in life had been difficult thanks to her parents and extended family. From all the information he'd gotten, she'd been in and out of child protective services until her grandmother stepped in. Once she did, Callie's life had been far easier, but still a struggle. She didn't come from money, and everything she got had to be earned.

Like rent.

That was where that fucking prick Sean Rigby entered her life. After her mother kicked her out of the grandmother's trailer on the same day of the funeral, Callie had been homeless. She'd probably needed rent money fast, and just looking at the cost of the rent for that piece of shit apartment, it was extortion. There was no way anyone would be able to make a life in that place. On the way upstairs, the stench alone had been enough to tempt him to expose her to the real him. The clubhouse was always busy with men coming and going, not to mention the abundance of women, but it was fucking clean and tidy.

The bank had turned her down for a loan, and so there was only one savior in her world at the time—Sean

Rigby, the local prick.

Brick sat outside of the loan shark's half-a-million-dollar house, located just out of town, not too far from the city.

It looked like a statement house. Purchased with dirty money.

Sean seemed to want the whole world to know he was coming up in the world. Callie had more than paid for her rental loan, but Sean kept on changing the rules to suit him, which explained the same sandwiches every single day. Peanut butter, and he noticed she always counted her change. Callie was his woman now, and that bullshit wouldn't cut it anymore.

Brick climbed off his bike. Tonight, he wore his leather cut.

He palmed his 9mm as he approached the gate. Two men puffed their chests out, looking so out of place.

"Move out of my way." His leather cut spoke volumes.

"You're not on the guest list," the first goon said.

He turned toward him and smiled. "Move." He was fast growing bored. With the blue balls he'd been living with, he wasn't in the mood to argue.

Arms folded, he looked at the two of them, ready to do some serious damage. They didn't move, and the second goon decided to reach for his piece.

Brick grabbed his wrist, twisted the man around, and had his arm snapped before the other guy even reacted. The moment his friend came at him, he slammed his fist in the man's face so hard, he collapsed to the ground. Brick's body wasn't ripped for show. He could handle himself in the worst of situations.

"I don't need to be on any fucking list." He spat on the ground, anger rushing through his body as he stepped past them, opening the gate. There was even a lock in place. He wrapped the chain around the fence, securing it in place so once those assholes were on their feet, there would be no way for them to interrupt him.

The key was in the lock, and he clicked it into place, taking the key with him. He placed it in his pocket and headed into the house. Only two more guards were in his way, and he took care of them without using his gun or knife.

Considering how many lives Sean Rigby had ruined, he figured the man would be clued in and have plenty of muscle to surround him.

There was no sign of Sean downstairs, and Brick slowly made his way up the winding staircase, drawing his gun. He had no doubt Sean knew how to handle himself. The man had come from nothing and rose up the ranks. Being a loan shark was just one of many side businesses. The man was dangerous. He had a history of making women who couldn't pay their debt work for him.

Prostitution was his main source of income, and the women had no choice but to earn for him. He preyed on the weak, exploited them, and it made him sick to his stomach just thinking about it.

The sounds of masculine groans came from the bedroom at the end of the hall. The door was partially open, and he saw Sean on his bed, a blonde between his thighs, sucking his cock. He had a hold of her hair in a death grip, forcing her to gag on his length.

"That's it, whore, take it deep. Sucking my dick takes a couple of dollars off your interest. Swallowing, well, that just gets you a few extra days."

Sean slammed his cock deep, and Brick knew the son of a bitch would make Callie do the same thing at some point. This was a power trip for him. Hurting women.

Brick had seen and heard enough. He kicked the door open, drawing his weapon as he looked at Sean. Brick wasn't some civilian off the street. He was VP of the Straight to Hell MC. Nobody wanted a visit from him.

The bastard groaned and shoved away the woman, who scrambled out of the room, running as fast as she could.

"You just interrupted a perfectly good blowjob," Sean said. He shook his head. "You can put that gun away."

"I like to hold it."

"Makes you feel powerful?" Sean asked. He reached for a pack of smokes. "You want one?"

"You know why I'm here."

"I've got no clue why a Straight to Hell MC is standing in my bedroom being a cock block. You just cost that woman some interest and a bit more time."

"This isn't a game," Brick said.

Sean laughed. "Wanna bet?"

Brick fired the gun, shooting the bed right between Sean's spread thighs.

"Another inch and that would be your dick. Lucky for you, I'm a good shot. Or am I?"

He saw the quiver in Sean's hand. The bastard wasn't half as calm as he claimed to be. "Callie. I want her debt removed immediately."

"That fat bitch owes me big, and I have a means to collect. Not happening. I've got no beef with you. Leave, and I'll call this even."

Brick smiled and tucked his gun away, but he didn't leave. He advanced toward the bed, grabbing Sean by the back of his head and slamming his palm down on his nose. The sound of bones crushing filled the air, as did Sean's screams.

THE BIKER'S DIRTY LITTLE SECRET

He was so fucking pissed. He pulled Sean from the bed and shoved him against the mirror. The glass broke from the impact.

He was surprised when Sean started to hit back, even with blood pissing from his nose. Brick blocked each hit and punched him in the face, getting him in the eye.

Each blow took Sean to the floor until he was in a heap, moaning and groaning.

Brick took his knife out and grabbed Sean's dick, which was now limp between his thighs.

"You're going to wipe Callie's slate clean, aren't you?"

"No, man, please don't."

His blade was fresh and sharp. He held the edge against the fucker's dick and waited for him to answer.

"Then answer me, or you're going to be living your life dickless. You won't be able to scare pussy with a fucking stump."

He was more than happy to take the guy's dick. It wasn't like he deserved it with the pain he'd caused. The more he thought about it, he'd be doing the rest of the world a favor.

"Yes, Callie's slate is wiped clean. No more loan. No nothing. I promise. She's small potatoes, anyway."

Brick was a little disappointed. Why couldn't the prick fight him a little more?

He removed his knife and wiped it on a clean towel. "Good answer. Pleasure doing business with you, Sean."

He whistled as he entered the bathroom, washing his hands before stepping back into the bedroom.

Sean tried to scramble away as fast as he could. Brick grinned.

He left the house without another word and found

the whore at the gate, shaking. With the key in hand, he slid it into the lock. The woman turned to him with a watery smile, thanking him.

He never answered, just climbed on his bike, taking one last look at the house. Callie deserved a nice place.

He had a sudden image of her pregnant with his child.

Never in all the years he'd been with the Straight to Hell MC, no, scrap that, in all the years he'd been a fucking adult, had he ever once thought of having a child.

Callie … what was it about this woman that made him forget his own personal vows to never bring a child into this world?

No woman had ever made him cave.

Callie was like no woman he'd ever met. She alone made him want everything. Rather than be angry, he smiled.

Today was a very good day.

****

The Skull Nation were coming around more and more. She spent a lot of time with her head down and was frequently sent off for breaks. Today, she had a nice little bump on her head for keeping to herself, walking into one of the steel posts that kept the main structure of the building up. Her head hurt, but she'd live.

She rubbed her temple with a moan and glanced around from her bench.

Brick hadn't called her in a couple of days.

They'd gone from being hot and heavy to him not calling. Was she a bad kisser? She didn't have anyone to compare her skill to. She'd never had the time for boys or men. Brick was different, though. He gave her this buzz, and every time she was around him, she felt like she was floating on cloud nine. It was the best feeling. She sipped at her coffee, feeling so incredibly tired. Her apartment had sprung a random leak last night, and glancing up at the sky, she knew the rest of the day was going to be a huge bust. Overnight, the bucket had filled countless times, and today she'd put out a larger one. There was no rainfall as yet.

The landlord refused to answer her calls.

Not to mention, Sean Rigby told her he'd be coming by for more of her money tonight. Well, interest. Her debt should have been paid in full by now. What had she been thinking getting messed up with a shady guy like him? Everything was so fucking messed up. She rubbed at her eyes.

When would the world give her one break? Just one? She wasn't even asking for much. All she wanted was some good luck to help her get through.

Lost in her own little worries and thoughts, she didn't realize Jeff had been calling her name. He stood in front of her, arms spread wide. "Are you going to come in and serve customers or what?" His voice rose, and she scrambled to her feet, rushing back into the shop to see a short line of customers.

Sporting a black eye, Jeff was limping a bit.

Things hadn't gone well with The Skull Nation MC. It wasn't her business, and working for him was starting to become a problem.

The Skull Nation pissed him off and upset him, and as payback, he often took it out on her. Normally, he was a decent guy, but in the last few weeks, he'd gotten meaner.

She finished serving the customers and stayed in the main shop, avoiding the back.

Time ticked by slowly, and when it was near to closing, Jeff came out of the back. He went to the front of the store, turned the sign over to closed, and locked the door.

"From now on, you stay in the shop. Don't leave it until it's your lunch break. Got it?"

"Yes," she said. He'd been the one to tell her to leave the store each time. Clearly, he wasn't happy with her following orders. "Jeff, is their business really worth this?"

He glared at her. "Are you trying to tell me how to run my store?"

She shook her head, swallowing hard. "No. Not at all." Callie held her hands up in submission so he knew she didn't mean anything bad about it.

"Just remember I gave you a job when no one would. You owe me, Callie. You should be fucking worshipping me. I stopped you from living a dog's life." He advanced toward her, and she cried out as he grabbed her arms and started to shake her. "You don't tell me what the fuck to do. Do you understand me?"

"Yes."

"Get it through your fucking skull. You work for me." He shoved her away, and she hit the side of the counter at a bad angle before falling to the tiled floor.

She cried out as pain exploded in her ribs.

"Get the fuck out of here before I fire you."

He stepped over her. The edge of his boot hit her as he moved. She didn't know if that was intentional or a mistake.

There was nothing she could do. She felt so small and desperate.

She needed this job.

Without another word, she grabbed her bag and jacket, then left the store immediately. The pain in her side wouldn't go away. She placed her palm down with a wince, pulling away.

THE BIKER'S DIRTY LITTLE SECRET

It was fine. She would look at it the moment she got home.

The walk to her apartment was slow going. She had no money for a taxi. With each passing second, the pain increased. At times, she had to stop in order to take a full breath.

The crash into the counter was bad. There was pain, and then there was this kind of pain.

Picking up her pace, she tried not to think about what this could mean. There was no way she'd go to the hospital. The cost alone would stop her from eating for months, and she'd end up homeless. Jeff didn't offer health insurance, so she had to be more careful.

With her apartment in sight, she breathed a sigh of relief.

The acrid stench of piss and feces assailed her when she opened the stairwell door.

She took one step in front of the other, making her way up the stairs. A working elevator would be heavenly about now. Perspiration dotted her brow. Each floor made her feel even crazier for living in this dump. There had to have been a better-priced ground-floor place somewhere.

Desperate times called for desperate measures, and with her mom kicking her out of the trailer without notice, she'd been pretty fucking desperate. Her grandmother had always told her to smile in the face of adversity, but right now, Callie felt more like curling up in a ball and giving up. Nothing she ever did was good enough. The little ray of light in her life, Brick, confused her.

She promised herself she'd never be a woman who waited around for a man to call. Brick had her always glancing at her cell phone. It was out of date, people teasing her for even having the relic, but she only ever had it in case of emergencies.

She got to her apartment door.

A sense of victory flooded her, and she placed her damp forehead against the wood. Her hands shook as she put the key in and opened her door.

Stepping inside, she turned on the light and screamed as she caught sight of Sean Rigby in her apartment, lounging on her sofa.

He looked ... a mess. Worse than Jeff ever looked. White tape was across his nose. Bruising all over his face, and the glare he directed her way, sent a shiver up her spine. She hadn't beat him up, but whoever did, well, they must have a death wish.

"Mr. Rigby," she said.

The pain wasn't going away. This wasn't good.

"Hello, Callie."

"I have your money, Mr. Rigby, but I wasn't able to go to the bank." She'd intended to go during her lunch break, but after Jeff had yelled at her, asking him if she could leave seemed wrong. She'd also gone without lunch. Now she was in pain and starving.

He got to his feet and advanced toward her.

Acrid fear filled her veins, and the adrenaline rush made her dizzy.

"Your debt is done," he said. "The next time you send a Straight to Hell MC piece of shit to my property, I won't be so forgiving."

She frowned. "I don't know what you're talking about." Straight to Hell MC. She'd never seen one of them. She heard of them, knew of their reputation—they were deadly. Most claimed they were worse than the Skull Nation.

"You have no idea, do you?" Sean asked.

She shook her head.

"Well, consider this payback. Maybe it's time for

THE BIKER'S DIRTY LITTLE SECRET

you to ask your boyfriend where he's from."

"Brick's a chicken farmer." Dots started to appear in front of her eyes. She felt out of control in her own body. The pain in her side had morphed into agony. The walk, and now this. It was all a little too much.

"You're such a fucking idiot. He's no chicken farmer. He's a fucking biker. The worst of the worst, and I should know. This is his handiwork." He pointed at his face. "I don't know what he sees in you. From what I heard, club pussy is rife where he comes from."

With that, he turned and left her apartment.

A Straight to Hell MC?

No, it wasn't possible.

Brick wouldn't lie to her.

Sean Rigby was the one who was lying.

She rushed to the mirror, or as fast as the pain would allow, stripped off her coat, and lifted her shirt. Bruises covered her ribs where she'd hit the counter, and she gasped.

How much damage could one little shove cause? She had the worse freaking luck.

There was no way she was going to avoid a hospital trip. Not as she suddenly felt dizzy. Sickness flooded her.

A knock at the door pulled her back to the present. She walked to it cautiously, wondering if Sean had changed his mind about her debt.

Opening the door, she frowned. Brick stood there, holding a bag, and the smells were amazing.

The world spun.

"Straight to Hell MC."

"Callie."

Why wouldn't the world stop spinning?

Closing her eyes, Callie allowed herself to be slumped into a black world where there was no pain.

Chapter Five

"Why am I here?" Lord asked.

They all looked out of place in the sterile hospital waiting room. His prez, Tank, and Reaper had come at his request.

"I told you about Skull Nation buying shit at the lumber yard, but there's more." He scrubbed a hand down his face. "Well, there's this girl. I think they beat her up. Maybe a warning or something?"

"I'm supposed to give a shit?"

"She's *my* girl."

Lord shook his head. "No, she's not. If you have a girl, I'd be the first to know. You're supposed to be my fucking VP, are you not?"

Brick paced, running a hand through his hair. "It's complicated."

"Is this why you've been sneaking off on your own the past couple of months?"

He nodded. "She doesn't know who I am. She's a civilian. Innocent."

"How could she not know? Look at you," Lord said.

"He's not wearing his cut," Reaper said.

"Why don't you shut the fuck up?" Brick had enough on his shoulders. As VP, he wouldn't think twice about teaching their enforcer some manners.

"Cool it. Both of you." Lord stared at him, that cold look that made most people piss their pants. "I was starting to wonder if you were the mole, moonlighting with the enemy. A chick, I can handle."

"I'd never betray you, Lord. I'd fucking die for the club." He glared at Reaper to punctuate the statement.

None of the hospital staff made a move to clear

them out of the hospital, even though they were loud and covered in ink. They wouldn't even make eye contact with them.

"So, what happened tonight?"

"I rode out to see Callie. It was supposed to be a quick visit. When I showed up, she'd been hurt bad. Last time I saw her, I may have sent a message to one of the Skull Nation, but they didn't know who I was. As far as they're concerned, I'm just a chicken farmer."

Tank snorted.

"What the fuck is happening?" Lord asked.

"It's a long story."

He wished he hadn't kept all this from Lord, but none of this was supposed to go so far. Callie was a forbidden pleasure, a walk on the other side of the fence. Then he fell hard for her without seeing it coming.

There was no backtracking now.

"And you want us to wipe out the Skull Nation in honor of your girl?" Reaper asked.

"No, I want you to go fuck yourself." Brick shoved the enforcer, one of the waiting room chairs falling back with an echo.

"Enough," Lord said. "What's her condition? She give you details?"

"I've only been here an hour or so. No one will tell me anything, and when I brought her in, she was in and out of consciousness."

"Find out."

Brick approached the main counter again. "I need an update on Callie Johnson."

The woman at the desk made a call, then pointed to the side doors. "A doctor is coming out to help you."

The automatic doors opened a few minutes later. Two doctors met them in the lobby.

"You're the one who brought in Ms. Johnson."

"Yes, tell me how she is," Brick insisted.

"She'll be fine. She has a pulmonary contusion—a bruised lung. We've already aspirated the fluid from her lungs and given her IV meds. It's a small impact area, so she'll recover quickly. Some painkillers and deep breathing exercises for a couple of weeks are all that she'll need."

"Is she awake?"

"Oh, yes, she's been awake for some time," said the doctor.

"When can she leave?"

"It's already late. I think it's best for her to rest here the night so we can monitor her. Tomorrow, she'll be discharged. Will you be able to pick her up, or is there someone else we need to contact?"

"I'll be here."

"Can he talk to her before we leave?" asked Lord.

The doctor nodded, urging him to follow. His prez told Reaper and Tank to wait for them in the lobby, then came along without being invited.

As they walked behind the doctors, Brick whispered, "She just found out about me. This is all new, and I know she'll be pissed."

"So you've lied to both of us."

"No, I didn't lie to anyone. I just didn't offer all the details."

"Same shit," Lord said. "You're VP because I trust you with my life. Don't let me down now, especially with all the talk that'll be going around the club now."

"I'm sorry," he said. "It wasn't supposed to go down like this. She wasn't supposed to matter."

"Until she did. Women have a way of doing that to a man. Are you sure she's the one?"

He didn't need to think twice. "A million

THE BIKER'S DIRTY LITTLE SECRET

percent."

"Okay then, let's make sure she's safe," Lord said.

They entered a room halfway down the hall. Callie was partially upright in the bed. Wires came from her arms.

"Brick."

He rushed over and carefully took her hand in his. "How you feeling, baby?"

"Better," she said. "I don't remember much."

Hopefully, she'd forgotten everything. Especially the part about the Straight to Hell MC.

"When you opened the door, you passed right out. I brought you to the hospital."

She frowned. "I can't afford this."

"Shit, Callie, don't worry about the bill. Just rest and get better."

The moment she noticed Lord behind him, she visibly tensed up. "Who's that?"

"He wants to know what happened to you. Who hurt you, Callie?"

"He's a biker," she whispered, looking at Lord.

Brick had to stop from smiling. She was so damn innocent and had no clue how fucked up he was. He wished he could live those two separate lives forever, but it wasn't possible. Eventually, he'd have to come clean, but was terrified she'd bolt.

"Nothing to worry about. Was it the Skull Nation? Don't be scared. He just needs to know."

She shook her head. "No, they never hurt me, just my boss. It was all an accident. He shoved me, and I hit the counter. He was just stressed. Jeff didn't mean it."

"Don't defend him."

Brick's jaw clenched. He remembered that little prick from the lumber yard. Maybe the truth coming out was for the best. For weeks, Brick wished Callie didn't have to work at that place or pinch pennies. If she lived at the club, he could take care of her. She wouldn't have to work or worry about a thing.

"Who's this Jeff guy?" asked Lord.

"Her boss."

"So, it wasn't the Skull Nation?"

"I guess not." He'd involved his prez and looked like a lying asshole for nothing. He should have waited until he'd talked to Callie.

Lord clapped him on the shoulder. "I'll meet you out front when you're done."

Once they were alone together, she squeezed his hand tighter.

"Brick, what are you doing getting involved with a guy like that? He's a biker. He's dangerous."

He chewed on his bottom lip, caught in the middle of a shitty situation of his own creation.

"*I'm* dangerous."

She shook her head. "You're not. I'm the one who got caught up in some bad business. Did Sean Rigby threaten you?"

"Baby, Sean Rigby is a small player, what we call a bottom feeder. You don't need to worry about him anymore."

She slid her hand away, gripping the edge of her blanket. "He said something about you. It's not true, though. I know it's not true."

"It's true. I'm the VP of the Straight to Hell MC."

Callie froze, then began breathing heavily, struggling to breathe. Her fucking monitors started beeping, and the doctors pushed their way in.

"Ms. Johnson, you have to breathe deeply."

Brick was ushered out of the room by a couple of nurses. He stood with his back to the wall until they'd

THE BIKER'S DIRTY LITTLE SECRET

stabilized her, then he quietly reapproached her bed.

"Callie?"

Her eyes were still closed when she spoke. "Was anything real? Was it all lies? Help me to understand this, Brick, because I sure don't."

"I did everything right, or so I thought. I'd do anything for you, Callie, but I can't change who I am. I knew once you found out about my sins, you'd walk the other way. I tried hard not to trip up, but the truth was bound to catch up with me."

"You assumed I'd walk. Maybe you should have been open with me. I'm not perfect, Brick. But I don't know what to believe now."

"Everything between us was real. The conversations, my feelings, all of it."

"Except who you are and where you come from. I just need time to think." She rolled away from him, effectively cutting him off.

Brick backed off, feeling completely at a loss. Would he be able to fix this? Would things ever be the same between them?

He met Lord back in the lobby, ready to face the music.

****

The next morning, she was able to shower and dress herself without much difficulty. She was sore, and it hurt to take a deep breath, but she'd live. Since she supposedly didn't have to pay back Sean Rigby, she had enough extra cash to take a taxi home. She didn't want to push herself with bus connections or walking miles just yet.

"Do you have someone picking you up?" asked her nurse.

"No, I'll be fine. I'm taking a taxi."

"I'll grab your discharge papers. Have you

already given your insurance to the accounting department?"

Callie shook her head.

"Well, you can do that before you leave." Once she left the room, panic surged inside her. How would this nightmare play out now?

First, her boyfriend was a wolf in sheep's clothing, and now she'd have a bill big enough to destroy any chance of a future. What more could go wrong?

She kept trying to think of excuses for Brick. If only things could go back to when she was blissfully in the dark about everything. Even when she'd refused to believe he was a biker, deep down, she knew he was. It was the lying that scared her. Her parents, cousins, and other relatives had all lied about everything growing up. Lying, cheating, and stealing were the norm. Callie didn't want her adult life to resemble anything like the dysfunction of her childhood.

She still couldn't believe Brick was a biker.

They were supposed to be violent, rude, and vulgar. But he was so good to her. Part of her was intrigued and a bit turned on. Why on earth was he dating a normal girl like her? Or was she one of many in his harem?

With all the questions in her head, she nearly forgot about her predicament. She was in a hospital without insurance. At least nothing was broken, but her prognosis still gave her a scare. She'd be sure to follow all the doctor's orders. Her real worry was when the bills would start coming in when she had nothing to pay them with.

With her discharge papers in hand, she headed to the accounting department to make some sort of arrangements for her bill. Why couldn't Jeff offer health insurance?

THE BIKER'S DIRTY LITTLE SECRET

She handed her papers to the clerk when it was her turn. They pulled up her information on the screen then handed her back the paperwork. "You're free to go. Hope you feel better."

"Will I just get a bill in the mail?"

The clerk frowned. "You're all paid in full."

Callie shook her head. "Sorry, I'm confused."

"You're free to go."

She stood up and didn't bother arguing. Callie walked, half in a daze, to the front entrance of the hospital. There were usually taxis waiting. How had her bill been paid in full? It had to be a massive bill for all the tests and care she'd received.

Then she saw *him.*

Brick was standing outside the old pick-up truck he'd used when they first met. When she thought he was a chicken farmer and things were so much simpler.

One thumb was hooked in his belt, the other hand resting on the truck. The man was hard and sexy, those dark eyes unraveling her. Why did things have to be so complicated?

Right away, she knew. He had to be the one who'd paid her bill. There was no one else in her life able or willing to do such a thing.

She walked down the main steps toward Brick. "Did you pay my bill?"

He shrugged.

"Brick, answer me. How much was it? I'll pay you back every penny."

"Don't worry about it." He reached out for her arm, holding her in place. "Are you okay? Feeling better?"

She took a breath. Callie had already fallen in love with Brick. Fallen hard. It was stupid to commit emotionally to a man so fast, but they were so alike, perfectly matched. Now she wasn't sure what was real and what was a lie.

"I feel much better. Just need to take it easy for a bit."

He nodded.

An awkward silence lingered between them.

They both attempted to speak at the same time, so they stayed quiet instead.

"Don't push me away, Callie."

"Brick, I don't even know what to say. You told me you were a chicken farmer."

"No, I never said that. You assumed," he said.

"And you could have corrected me." She pulled away from his grip. "I should go."

She only made it a few steps away when his voice, at full volume, stopped her in his tracks. "I'm only human!"

Callie turned to face him.

"I was good enough for you before, but I'm the same man, Callie." He held both arms out to the sides. "I'm a sinner. You can't love a sinner?"

"Brick, quiet." She rushed over to him and gave him a little shove in the chest, loving the feel of him. "People are looking."

"I don't give a shit. All I care about is you."

"Then why did you lie about who you were?"

He looked down at her, his features set hard. "Because of this. You're judging me. If I could have kept the truth from you forever, I would have. I don't want you thinking less of me, Callie."

"I don't think less of you. I just want to know what's real between us. Bikers don't exactly have the best reputation."

"Everything between us was real. All of it. You're the reason I want to get out of bed in the

THE BIKER'S DIRTY LITTLE SECRET

morning. Why do you think I've been replaying first base for months? Because I'm a player? No, because I respect you and want you to see that."

She didn't know what to say. Her emotions and sense of logic were tearing her down the middle. Who was she to judge? Most of her family tree could be framed with mug shots.

"What happens now, Brick?"

"Just don't leave."

"You're dangerous. How can I make a future with you?"

"You think I'd ever hurt you, baby?"

"I don't know what to think anymore," she said. "I want to believe things will work, but I'm scared."

"Say you'll give me a chance. I'll show you how good things can be."

He'd already shown her. She had more happy memories built up with Brick than she had with her own family over a lifetime. He'd even come to her work with a picnic lunch one afternoon, complete with the checkered blanket. Everything he did or said made her feel like a princess. The man was so thoughtful and protective. How could he be a criminal?

Tears filled her eyes because she didn't want to lose him. She just wished things were easier, but since when had anything in her life been simple?

"I was upset you hid the fact you're part of the Straight to Hell MC. I'm still in shock, to be honest."

"I'm not a monster."

"I know." She cupped the side of his face, loving the feel of his rough stubble. "Promise you won't lie anymore?"

He nodded.

"Who was that guy you brought to the hospital yesterday?"

"The president of our club. I've been keeping things from him too, thinking I was protecting you. But he's been pretty understanding. His old lady was a civilian, too."

"This is a lot to take in."

Maybe it wouldn't be so bad being in a relationship with a biker. Brick got Sean Rigby to back off, and he always defended her when the Skull Nation got too close. Everything was starting to make sense as she thought back to countless incidents that should have made her question things. What kind of chicken farmer had that much ink? She must have kept herself in the dark rather than seeking the truth.

"Come on, I'm driving you home."

Her instinct was to argue, but she bit her tongue and let him open the door for her. Once he was in the driver's seat, they were off. "No bike today?"

"I don't want to hurt you. What you need is some rest."

"I guess."

He watched the road, silence filling the cab of the truck.

"Jeff needs to be dealt with."

"What? What are you talking about?"

"Callie, he hurt you. I can't leave that alone."

She began to panic. Callie didn't want Brick to do something stupid and get into trouble, and she couldn't lose her job because her boyfriend crossed the line with Jeff.

"Just leave it alone, okay? It was an accident. Ever since the Skull Nation have been around buying supplies, he's been on edge. I know they've beat him up on more than one occasion."

"You want me to feel sorry for that piece of shit? You're mine, Callie. He never should have put his filthy

THE BIKER'S DIRTY LITTLE SECRET

hands on you."

"I'll deal with it. I'm sure he'll have forgotten all about what happened on my next shift."

"You're actually going back there?"

"I have rent and bills to pay, Brick. I don't have the luxury of walking away from that job." Tears threatened to take over again. A frog built up in her throat. "I'm twenty-six years old, I've never been to college, and before I got that job, I was homeless without a penny to my name. I *need* that job."

"You think too little of yourself. The whole world is yours. You can be anything, Callie."

"Those are just pretty words."

"Then you think too little of me," he said. "Don't underestimate my reach."

Chapter Six

Brick had every intention of dropping Callie off and going to deal with her boss. Instead, one look inside her pitiful apartment, and he knew what he needed to do. While she rested on the sofa, he called the boys at the clubhouse and told them to get everything ready for him. He was coming back home and bringing his woman with him. She'd have full round-the-clock care, and it meant she could start to get used to being around him and the club.

He made her a coffee and disappeared into her bedroom, packing away her paltry belongings. The clothes she wore weren't suitable. Most of them looked like they'd been purchased from thrift stores and should have gone straight into the trash. Holes, and he saw stitch mark after stitch mark.

His woman wasn't going to be dealing with second-rate belongings anymore.

Still, until he got the time to go shopping with her, he packed what he thought was suitable for the club. Some of the brothers just needed to see a little slither of skin and were ready to fuck.

Damn, this was a fucking nightmare. For a woman like Callie to capture his attention, she was going to be the spectacle of the year. The guys were going to be ribbing him about this for months, and the women, he didn't even want to think about them.

They were all going to be told she was off-limits.

She was his woman.

There was no way he'd allow anyone else to go near her or to fucking touch her. She belonged to him and him alone.

With a case packed, he returned to the living

THE BIKER'S DIRTY LITTLE SECRET

room, finding Callie with her eyes closed.

He walked closer, and she opened them. "Hey," she said.

Her gaze fell to the bag. "Are you stealing my stuff?"

"No, you're coming with me."

"Brick, I'm really tired."

"This isn't a request. You're coming with me whether you like it or not."

Her eyes went wide. "Brick, don't."

"You either walk to the car, or I'll carry you. The choice is yours, and you've got less than a minute to make it."

"I'm not leaving my place."

"Ten ... nine ... eight..."

"You can't be serious?" she asked.

"Seven ... six..."

She got to her feet, and he was a little gutted as he'd hoped she'd pick a different path. He would've loved a reason to have her body pressed up against his.

Callie was a strong woman. She was clearly in pain, but she hid it. The pinched lips and stilted gaze gave it away. He wanted to take the pain from her.

Following close behind, they walked down to his car. He helped her inside before throwing her suitcase in the back.

It was a long drive back to the clubhouse.

Neither of them spoke for the longest time.

"I didn't want you to freak out about me," Brick said.

"Why do you think I would've done that?"

"Before I got a chance to say who I was or what I did, you already made assumptions, Callie. I tried to hide it all because I didn't want to expose you."

"You can't be like that," she said. "I'm not weak.

I can handle anything."

He glanced over to see her rubbing at her temple.

"Babe, you passed out."

"I was in pain. Jeff had hurt me." She shrugged. "It was no big deal."

"Why do you justify men hurting you?"

"I'm not. I mean, I know it sounds like it, but I don't mean to. I need this job." She blew out a breath. "You wouldn't understand."

"Why?"

"Because … I don't know. You're a guy, and it's different in this world for you. I'm a woman."

"You're playing the sexist card?"

"Were you hoping I'd play the 'you're a criminal card' and say you've never done an honest day's work in your life?" she asked. "I know for a fact you're a hard worker."

"Oh, yeah, and what makes you think that?" he asked.

"Your hands."

He glanced down at his hands gripping the steering wheel. "My hands?"

"Yeah. Someone who doesn't work hard has smooth, baby-soft hands. You have calloused hands. I don't know what you do, but you work hard. I'm not going to insult you, Brick."

"But you want to play the sex card?"

"Tell me I'm wrong."

He stared out of the window.

She chuckled.

"What?" he asked.

"I had no idea what it would take to get you to be quiet."

"There are a lot more fun ways to get me to be quiet and have you screaming for more." He chanced a look at her and saw her face had flamed.

"You can't say stuff like that," she said.

"Why not?"

"Because..."

"You don't have a reason, and I want you to know that this changes nothing. You're still mine, Callie."

"But are you mine?" she asked.

"Always."

He pulled into the clubhouse parking lot and went to the first available spot. After climbing out, he went straight to Callie's side, helping her and grabbing her case. Then, with several of the guys and club pussy mingling outside, he guided her up to the main building.

Lord waited inside.

The smirk on his face made him want to put his punch it off. Instead, he offered a tight smile and an even glare.

"I didn't think it could be true." Ally, Lord's old lady, broke through the tension. The other woman rushed forward. "I'm Ally. When Lord said that Brick had a woman and was bringing her here, I was so excited. Brick doesn't like me very much, but I think we're going to get along really well."

"Ally, baby, let Brick get her settled."

"Oh, right. We'll talk soon."

Callie offered a tight smile and followed Brick through the main clubroom, going toward the stairs.

"Who was that?" Callie asked.

"That was Lord's old lady. Whatever you do, don't insult her. She never used to talk so much, but since they've gotten married and had a kid, well, things have been, how do I say this, chatty. She won't shut up."

"She has a child?"

He nodded.

"Oh."

"We all live like civilized people here. We're not heathens."

"Right. Right. I'm sorry. This is all a little surreal. I guess your place looks kind of normal."

He snorted. "What did you think? We'd have sacrificial virgins, or drugs spread out across the table?"

"I don't know. You hear so much bad news about biker gangs. I judged you before knowing anything. I'm sorry," she said.

He stopped outside his door and placed a finger beneath her chin, forcing her to look up at him. "Don't be sorry."

"I ... I don't want you to hate me."

"That is never going to be possible." He pressed a kiss to her lips. "I like you way too much." He flicked his tongue across her lips and she opened up.

Brick had no choice but to pull back. With her in his room, sleeping in his bed, this was going to prove to be stressful for him. He would need to show some restraint, even though all he wanted to do was fuck her hard and fast. She needed time to recover.

Once inside, he stepped back to allow her space to enter.

"You need to rest. I've got a couple of errands to run. Do you want some food?"

"No, I'm not hungry."

"I'll bring some back when I've finished. This is your home now," he said.

"Brick, I can't stay here. I've got a life and plans."

"We'll talk."

She didn't need to think about the future right now. She just needed to accept him and their time together.

THE BIKER'S DIRTY LITTLE SECRET

Callie may not know it yet, but he owned her. She belonged to him, and there was nowhere else for her to go.

He pressed a kiss to her head, then showed her the en-suite bathroom. A couple of rooms on the floor beneath them had to share one. There was no way he was going to let anyone see her naked. That privilege would be for him and him alone.

"I'll be back."

"What are you going to do?" she asked.

"Some club errands. I'll be back before you know it."

He kissed her head again and headed out of the room. Leaving her was so fucking hard. Walking downstairs, he saw Lord was already waiting for him.

"Ally wants to meet her. She's really excited."

"Soon," he said.

"We going to fuck this guy up?"

"You got it."

He headed out to his bike and was surprised Lord, Stump, and Reaper followed him.

"What are you guys doing?" he asked.

"Do you think you're the only one going to have the fun giving a message not to fuck with the Straight to Hell MC?" Lord asked.

"Yeah, let's go and fuck with some assholes," Reaper said.

Stump climbed on his bike.

"You've got the whole backing of the club, Brick. You're not alone," Lord said.

He breathed deep. He wasn't going to cry like a fucking pussy. But, right now was a reminder of why he was so fucking loyal to his club. They were a family.

"Let's do this." He straddled his bike, turned it on, and allowed the engine to purr to life. It felt so fucking good hearing the sound.

This was his life, and he wanted Callie to become part of it.

They took off, heading toward the address he'd gotten from Stitch. It was where he'd find Jeff. The fucker lived in a really nice house in a decent neighborhood, and he had a feeling Skull Nation MC had a lot to do with that.

They pulled up to the country house. For a guy who owned a hardware store, he certainly had a nice place. Brick knew deep down something else was going on here. The hardware store and lumber yard wasn't even a chain. It was a single store in a town barely on the map. He needed to look into Jeff.

Brick climbed off his bike as Jeff came to the front door.

"I suggest you think twice about whatever it is you're going to do. I'm protected," he said.

Interesting.

He didn't stop moving forward. Jeff had a bat in his hand.

"Do you want me to use this?"

Please do.

"Do you think I'm going to let you get away with hurting my woman?" he asked.

Jeff paled. "You need to leave."

"And you need to learn not to mess with my business." He drove his fist into the guy's face.

Callie had asked him not to mess with her boss. Well, she wasn't going back to work, regardless. He'd take care of her and all of her plans.

****

Hunger hit Callie hard and she rubbed at her stomach.

Brick said he'd bring food back, but she was

THE BIKER'S DIRTY LITTLE SECRET

starting to feel a little sick, and with the medication she'd been given, they had told her to eat. Now she was in pain, hungry, and achy. She wouldn't take any medication without food.

Settling down onto the bed, she felt the comfort of the mattress beneath her. It was a nice bed. It smelled like Brick.

She smiled to herself, giving it a little bounce as she did.

There was no risk of bed bugs or rodents here, or even cockroaches. She released a shiver just thinking about her place. No matter how hard she cleaned or decorated, her place seemed to always have a problem, from the damp to the bugs.

Tucking her hair behind her ears, she lay back and snuggled up to a pillow. It didn't smell like him, and seeing as she was alone, she reached for his pillow, pressing it against her face and breathing in.

This smelled like him, and she couldn't wipe the smile off her face.

Smoothing out the fabric, she breathed a sigh of relief. She'd already kicked her shoes off and taken a shower. Her hair was dry, and she was bored.

Hungry. Bored. Tired.

But the doctor's orders said to rest, so she had to get used to this for a little while.

How had she found herself in the Straight to Hell MC's clubhouse? She promised herself years ago she'd never get mixed into this kind of crowd.

The memory of her life before her grandmother had taken her bombarded her. The cops making late-night visits. The way they treated them like trash. She hated all of it.

Her grandmother had shown her another life, even though modest, with the warning to stay on the straight and narrow.

She ran fingers through her hair. Would her grandmother like Brick? He wasn't like her parents, or even her two brothers.

With her face pressed into Brick's pillow, she breathed in deeply, only to panic, releasing a squeal, when the door opened.

She quickly looked to see Brick struggling with a large box of food.

His gaze was averted, and she quickly put his pillow back, hoping he hadn't caught her breathing in his scent like a crazy person. What kind of woman sniffed a guy's pillow? She was going crazy.

He kicked the door closed and turned toward her.

"Hey, beautiful," he said.

"Hey." His compliments always took her by surprise. She wasn't used to men finding her attractive. "Did you finish running your errands?"

"Yep. All done." He put the food on the bed. "You know, anytime you want the real thing, I'm right here."

"Real thing?"

He winked at her as he looked at the pillow.

She immediately covered her face. "You saw that?"

"Kind of hard to miss."

She groaned. "No. You can't say stuff like that. It's not very nice."

"What? I can't say that I love seeing you cuddling with my pillow and it made me hot as hell?" he asked.

Heat filled her cheeks. Did he really mean that or was he just saying it to be nice?

Silence fell between them. She didn't know what to say or do.

"I got us food. I hope you love Chinese food."

"I do." She gave him a smile, hoping he knew she appreciated him not making her feel any more embarrassed than she usually felt. "I'm starving."

"And I'm here to feed you." He gave her a wink, removed his leather cut, and took a seat on the bed. "Have what you want."

He opened a carton, and she watched him grab an egg roll out, taking a large bite out of it. "So good."

Her mouth watered, and she chose a spring roll. "You got so much food."

"I had no idea what you liked."

She giggled. "Look at me, I like most foods."

"Don't do that anymore. I don't like it."

"Do what?"

"You know what you were doing. Stop putting your weight down. I don't like it. All of it."

She picked up another carton and some chopsticks. The scent of fragrant noodles was intoxicating. "I'm just ... I guess I'm used to it. It's easier to make fun of yourself when everyone else seems to do it."

"Don't get used to it. It doesn't suit you."

She nibbled on her lip. After men like Jeff in her life, and pretty much most men she'd met, she wasn't used to any of them complimenting her. Liking her the way she was without insisting she needed to lose weight to look pretty.

Brick ate his food, and she liked watching him dig in without a care in the world. She slurped up her noodles, and he opened up another carton, presenting her with a piece of fried tofu. He'd dipped it into a spicy sweet and sour sauce. "You've got to try this."

She took a bite, eyes closed, and hummed her appreciation. "So good."

"Yeah, you've got that right."

They finished most of the food, and Brick took the remainder down to the kitchen. He came back with a glass of water for her to take her pain pills.

"How about I take a shower and then we sit and watch a movie?"

"If you'd like to?"

"Yes," he said.

She watched him tug his shirt off over his head, presenting her with his heavily inked back. Callie held her breath as a wave of desire swirled through her body. He disappeared into the bathroom.

Nerves hit her hard.

Alone with Brick in his room, watching a movie. Could she do this?

She already wore a pair of pajamas, and she quickly scrambled beneath the covers. The sound of the water running and the occasional grunt drew her attention. At first, she tried to ignore the sounds, but they kept on coming.

She pushed off the blanket and stepped away from the bed. With one foot in front of the other, she moved closer toward the door, praying the floor didn't creak. The sounds grew louder.

The door was open wide enough for her to look through without making a sound.

I shouldn't be doing this.
This is his private room.
Go back to bed.
Don't be rude.

She glanced around the door, and at first, she couldn't make out what was going on. Slowly, she saw. The curtain didn't hide much, and it was clear exactly what he was doing.

His fist was wrapped around his cock, working up and down the length. The heavy sounds of his grunts

THE BIKER'S DIRTY LITTLE SECRET

filled the air, and she quickly pulled back from the door.
Why was he masturbating?
Was he thinking about her?
Other people?
There were plenty of willing and available women for him to claim around here.
Jealousy struck her hard, and she went back to the bed.
Seconds passed, even minutes.
She kept on waiting, and finally, after what felt like a lifetime, he came out. He had a towel wrapped around his waist. There was more ink on his chest and abdomen. She even caught sight of some on his legs. It surprised her how much it aroused her.
"You know, you don't have to be embarrassed."
"What?"
"I was thinking of you," he said.
"Oh, you saw me?" Callie wanted to die right there.
"Babe, I've lived my life while constantly watching my back. Believe me, I notice everything."
Her cheeks felt like they were on fire. "I ... I didn't mean to spy."
"I've got no problem with you watching me. I would've liked you to come in and join me."
"Brick, I'm not like that," she said.
"Like what?"
She didn't want him to think she was like the women at the club, ready to do anything a man wanted. Her nerves picked up. What if he really thought of her that way?
"I'm not used to ... men ... you know."
"Not used to men thinking about fucking you while taking a shower?"
She shook her head.

He threw his towel into the bathroom and then dropped the one around his waist. She quickly averted her gaze as he moved to the other side of the bed and slid beneath the sheets. She didn't know if he'd put on a pair of shorts or boxers.

"Look at me, Callie."

She glanced at him and looked away.

"Come on. You know me."

She finally looked at him. "Do I?"

"Everything about me is the same. The only part of me that has changed is me being part of the Straight to Hell MC. This club is my life. It's my family. I didn't want to lie to you in the beginning, but I didn't want to let you down. You'd made your assumptions. Like everyone does. I had no idea where this was going, and why would I want to mess it up?" He reached out to tuck a stray curl behind her ear. "You're beautiful, perfect, and most importantly, you're all mine."

His possessive nature shouldn't arouse her, but it sure as hell did.

She tentatively touched his cheek. She stroked her thumb back and forth. He hadn't shaved, and there was some stubble growth.

"I'm all yours, Callie," he said.

She wanted that to be true. She'd never wanted anything so much in her life. "People always leave me."

"Not me. I'm not going anywhere."

THE BIKER'S DIRTY LITTLE SECRET

Chapter Seven

Three weeks later

His world felt complete. Callie was safe under his wing, and there was no need to hide their relationship from Lord. Brick couldn't be happier.

Callie was taking a shower, so he was killing some time outside. Being in the next room, knowing she was naked and sudsy only feet away, tested his control too much. They'd celebrated their three-month anniversary recently. It was the longest he'd gone without passing first base. He usually fucked them and left them on day one, but until Callie, no woman had ever mattered.

He was shining the chrome on this bike when he noticed the set of black boots stop next to him, a bit of dust whirling up.

"Our guy at city hall said the Skull Nation just got utilities hooked up at their new clubhouse," said Copper.

Brick was VP, so despite his obsession with Callie, he still had a job to do.

"They build it, we tear it down," Brick said. "Rally the boys. We'll do a ride by then go hard and heavy tonight. We'll burn them to the fucking ground. It'll be déjà vu for those motherfuckers."

"I'll let them know."

He'd likely take Reaper and Tarmac with him for the first run. Brick wanted to scope out the area and get a feel for what they were dealing with. That little pussy, Jeff, had squealed like a pig when he'd paid him a visit, giving away a lot of Skull Nation secrets.

"Hey," Brick called as Copper walked away.
"Yeah?"

"Any progress on Lord's rat? You know how much he hates them, and he's riding my ass."

"Somewhat. There's a signal from inside the club—a camera, tracker, phone tap, something."

"And?"

"Well, it's not as easy to pinpoint the exact location. I'm working on it."

Brick massaged his temples. "If the device is in front of you, would you know?"

Copper shrugged. "I could use a scanner, well, build one, but—"

"Do it. As soon as you're done, you let me know and I'll get all the boys in church with their phones. We'll try to root out whoever's selling secrets."

"Will do."

Brick tossed his rag and headed back upstairs. He wanted to spend some time with Callie before he rode off on business again.

He opened the bedroom door just as she walked toward the bed, a towel wrapped around her hair and another around that curvy body. The room smelled like lavender and vanilla. He'd bought her everything she'd requested weeks ago. It was important for her to feel at home and have everything her heart desired.

"You startled me," she said. Her smile always brightened a room. Callie was his shining star in the club, and her sweet innocence had a healing effect on him.

"I have to head out in about an hour, but I won't be long."

"Something wrong?"

He shook his head. Brick never wanted her to worry about anything. That was his job.

"Will we still be able to go to the river?"

Brick had promised to take Callie on a hike to the river a few miles from the clubhouse. He'd often head down there when he needed to clear his head. She wanted to get closer to him, and as hard as it may be, he had to open up to her more.

"If not today then tomorrow, for sure."

She sat on the edge of the bed and towel dried her long hair. Even fresh out of the shower, she was perfect. Brick watched her, completely mesmerized by her beauty. He couldn't stand women with a face full of makeup. Callie was all natural, in every way. A few times her towel would slip, and she'd tuck up back up under her arms.

For nearly a month, they'd slept in the same bed. It wasn't easy being a gentleman. He felt like a fucking superhero for refraining this long. Every time her soft curves rubbed up against him, his cock would react. He'd spent a lot of time pleasuring himself in the shower, but there was only so much a man could take.

"You smell good." He sat next to her and kissed her shoulder. "How you feeling?"

"I told you last week, I feel like I'm back to normal."

"You're sure?"

"Yes, Brick, you can stop worrying about me." Callie turned to face him, trailing a single finger down the center of his chest. "I'm fine. Promise."

He gritted his teeth. Even her innocent touch drove him feral with need.

Maybe it was the mood in the room or the need in his eyes, but she became quiet, only the sound of their breathing to break the hush. He leaned forward, slowly, and gently brushed his lips to hers.

"You said you were a virgin."

She nodded.

He kissed her again. "Will you give yourself to me? Make me your man?"

Callie's body physically tensed, but she didn't pull away. "I'm already yours."

She ran her hand down his arm, testing his muscles.

"Not yet."

Brick wasn't used to good girls. She was either too shy to say yes or nervous to give him the green light. But one thing for sure, she wasn't pushing him back. He needed to take the lead or this would never happen. He *needed* it to happen.

"Let me touch you, baby." He whispered the words against her neck. Her skin was still damp and fragrant. He trailed kisses along her skin, gently unraveling her towel with his free hand. It fell down to her lap, exposing her beautiful, sloping tits. He groaned. His cock ached to be freed, but he focused on Callie's needs. This was her first experience. He'd be her first man. There was something uniquely satisfying knowing she belonged only to him.

Brick didn't take that honor lightly. Knowing he'd be the first to taste her, fuck her, pushed his territorial instincts off the charts.

He used the backs on his knuckles to caress the side of her breast. Her skin was soft and supple. She shivered under his touch.

"Brick." She barely breathed out the word, a throaty sound filled with need.

"Relax, Callie. Let me make you feel good. So fucking good."

He put any thoughts of business of out his mind and devoted himself one hundred percent to his woman.

She tugged him closer, wrapping her arms around his neck. "I've been thinking about this day for a long time," she said.

"Really?" He ran his tongue along the shell of her

THE BIKER'S DIRTY LITTLE SECRET

ear, earning him a moan.

Callie nodded. "When you work out, sometimes I hope you'll start something."

Why hadn't she said anything? Knowing she was attracted to him and ready to move forward in their relationship only spurred him on. Brick hit the gym religiously, and now that Callie lived at the club, she'd hang out and watch him. He had no idea she was really thinking.

"Good to know." He tugged off his t-shirt, then crawled over her, forcing her to lay back. They did a quick roll until they were in the middle of the bed. Her playful squeal was adorable. She ran her hands all over his chest and shoulders. "You drive me crazy," he said.

He kissed her hard on the mouth, and nothing else mattered but the two of them. She was so receptive, her little tongue sliding against his as the kiss deepened. Never in his life had he felt this way for a woman. For anyone. He couldn't get enough of her. And he knew he'd *do* anything for her.

When he finally pulled away, she whined, reaching for him. He didn't leave, only tossed her damp towel, leaving her nude over the made bed. She tried to hide against him, but Brick wanted to see it all.

"You being shy with me now, Callie?"

She shrugged.

"Never hide yourself from me. There's no reason to. I love everything I see, baby."

He moved down her body, grateful for the daylight coming in the window. Brick circled her areola with his tongue, then sucked her tit into his mouth. He alternated between her breasts, continuing his descent. As he nipped her sides, kissing and exploring, he spread those thick thighs.

Her breathing picked up, her fists grabbing

handfuls of blankets.

"Such a pretty pussy." Her folds were pink and glistening with arousal. A dusting of fair hair over her mound. He licked his lips. "I'm going to make you come with my mouth, Callie. I want to hear you scream."

****

Callie would be lying if she said she hadn't been fantasizing about this day. Only she hadn't expected it to feel this damn good. Brick wasn't holding back. As he spread her thighs, she fought to keep them closed. He wasn't having it. Her natural instinct was to hide herself. She feared if he saw the real her, he'd change his mind about their relationship.

Now that he'd seen everything and kept on going, she felt a unique sense of relief and freedom. She didn't have to deny herself any longer.

Tonight, she'd lose her virginity to a biker. The Straight to Hell VP. It was all surreal. But sex was one thing. A lasting connection required so much more. They had attraction, friendship, romance, and intimacy—but he didn't know the real her. And she didn't know the real Brick. Until they shared more about who they were, this was all just fun and games.

Callie was falling in love with Brick. Every time she saw him, her heart raced. He made her feel alive, beautiful, and safe. Her entire world was morphing into something new—no more shitty apartment, no more pinching pennies, no more dealing with Jeff's mood swings.

Her thoughts were drowned out when Brick's mouth came down over her pussy, his tongue flicking her clit until she was arching off the mattress. He was filthy and determined to make her see stars. She never thought she'd enjoy something like this, but he made it feel like raw ecstasy. Callie peered down and saw his broad, inked shoulders and part of his back as he devoured her pussy. She loved his body, every hard, muscular inch. It was one of the reasons she felt insecure being with him. Any woman would dream to be with a man like him. And the club was overrun with half-naked, beautiful women.

His hands slid under her ass, keeping her in place as he rubbed his face against her folds. He was enjoying this as much as she was. When he settled over her sensitive clit, suckling her without reprieve, the pressure began to build deep in her core.

"Brick!"

He didn't stop, rather began flicking his tongue faster until she was writhing on the bed like a madwoman. The orgasm came barreling forward like a freight train, crashing in a blinding release. This was all new, and she imagined she'd become addicted to everything Brick after today.

She was a puddle on the bed, her breathing still heavy. Everything was a blur, and she vaguely remembered screaming Brick's name. As the intensity of the moment died down, she became hyperaware of everything around her. She was scared to open her eyes and embarrass herself.

Callie finally peeked open one eye, only to find Brick smiling at her.

"You screamed my name."

"Did I?"

He bit his lip, and it was the sexiest thing she'd ever seen. "I wouldn't forget a thing like that." Brick winked then cupped her cheek, kissing her mouth, taking her under again.

He began unbuckling his belt without breaking the kiss. As much as she was nervous to lose her virginity, she was ready. More than ready. Her pussy was still tingling from coming all over his face.

"I want you so bad, baby. I want to come deep in your cunt. Make you mine."

Why did his filthy mouth only turn her on more?

"Yes." It was all she could manage.

He kicked off his jeans and mounted her. She didn't dare look down to see his bare cock. Just the outline of him flaccid in his workout shorts was enough to give her pause. He wasn't a small man in any way. He was power, strength, and virility combined.

She gasped as he dry thrust against her bare mound with his erection. Damn, he was hard, like a heavy lead bar pressed against her more sensitive parts.

"Relax for me, baby. I'll try to go nice and slow."

She hadn't realized her nails were gripping both his shoulders in a death grip. He didn't seem to care.

He positioned himself at her entrance, easily pushing in the thick tip. She was soaked, helping him ease his cock inch by inch into her virgin hole. Callie was starting to think she'd be a virgin for life. Once he filled her balls deep, he paused to kiss her neck and nip her ear. She tested her muscles around his erection. She couldn't believe he was inside her. Sex may mean nothing to him, but it meant something special to Callie. A new bond seemed to forge between them the moment he penetrated her.

"Fuck you're tight." He whispered the words against her skin, followed by a masculine groan. In order to give him permission to continue, she wriggled beneath him. She wanted more, wanted to feel him claiming her, fucking her hard.

He deserved his own release after what he'd just given her.

And what kind of man, a biker no less, played the role of a gentleman for this long without walking out the door? He was something special, and all hers.

THE BIKER'S DIRTY LITTLE SECRET

He began to pull out and slide back in, slow and steady, testing, moving with caution.

"You're not hurting me, Brick. Please, I need you."

His mouth claimed hers again, kissing her hard and desperate. Simultaneously, he began fucking her harder, one hand under her ass so he could fill her even deeper.

"I love you, Callie." He fucked her harder, faster, a sheen of sweat forming between their bodies as they collided.

She pondered his words. Were they said in the heat of the moment? Did they mean more? Could he love her? Callie had never known the love of a man. She craved Brick's devotion, but didn't want to assume a thing, especially now.

His erection was like silk over steel, and the way he filled her was pure satisfaction. Every thrust of his hips made her gasp and mewl. She was completely wanton, and there was no stopping it. She wrapped her arms around his neck, pleading for more in his ear.

"Come for me, Callie. Come all over my cock."

She closed her eyes and savored the illicit pleasure, never wanting it to end. Her orgasm was on a precipice.

"Be a good girl. Come for me, baby."

This time, she let go, wave after wave of release washing through her. Her breath came out in small shudders as the enormity of her orgasm shook her to the core. She felt the moment he came inside her.

His weight came down on her briefly, but he immediately returned his weight to his arms, then rolled to the side.

"That was worth the wait," he said, an arm draped over his eyes. The man looked so edible, she wouldn't complain if he wanted to claim her again.

"And it wasn't scary at all."

He shifted to his side, his eyes narrowed as he looked at her. "You were scared? Why?"

"I've never done it before. I wasn't sure what to expect."

"Did it hurt?" he asked.

She shook her head. "I loved it."

That earned her a smile.

"What happens now?" she asked, feeling vulnerable now that her virginity was no longer at play. A small part of her worried he'd walk once he got what he wanted, which didn't make sense. He was too good to her.

"What do you mean?" He tucked hair behind her ear. They were face-to-face on the bed, both naked and exhausted.

"Do things change? This feels like a big step."

"Nothing changes," he said. Her heart instantly dropped. "I was already loyal to you from the first day. Sex doesn't change that. I'm yours, and now you're all mine."

"And we'll talk more … when you take me to the river?"

"Yeah. I promised we'd talk, and we will."

She hoped things didn't change when he learned the ugly truth about her past, although he knew many details and was still here. It was almost as if he liked that she was normal, average, and low maintenance. The opposite to women at the club.

"You know some things about me," she said.

"It's my job to keep the club safe. I had to be sure you weren't a threat."

"And?"

"Squeaky clean." He touched the tip of her nose.

THE BIKER'S DIRTY LITTLE SECRET

"You sure about that?" she asked.

He scoffed. "Compared with my life, you're a saint, baby."

"I don't know anything about you, Brick. Not a thing."

"Know that I'll do anything for you. Isn't my devotion enough?"

She swallowed hard. "Of course, it is, but I still want to know you. I don't want secrets between us."

"It's not secrets I'm worried about. It's just that sometimes the past is better left buried. And some of the shit I have to handle for the club is too ugly to talk about. I won't soil your mind with all that bullshit. I won't."

"Can I know a little about you? Relationships can't be based on sex alone. What about when you were a boy? About your family?"

He visibly cringed.

"I'm sorry."

"We both got the short stick in the parent department, but we deal with it, right?"

She nodded.

"I've never shared any details of my childhood with anyone, not even Lord. But we'll talk at the river. I want you to believe me when I say I'm serious about you, about us."

"I wish I could know everything."

"No, you don't want that, trust me." He took her hand, forcing her to trace a faint white line on his pec. It was slightly raised and jagged.

"What's this from?" She expected it to be from a rival biker.

"My mother."

Her breath caught in her throat, and he was right, she didn't want to know. Her parents had been junkies and petty criminals, but they'd never hurt her like that.

Mostly, she dealt with neglect rather than physical abuse.

"She was pissed off my father left us. Blamed me. Called me a worthless piece of shit who'd ruined her life," he said. "I thought she'd be happy because he used to beat her, you know. But I guess some women are too fucked up to see their relationships are self-destructive."

"Brick..."

"See, you're feeling sorry for me. Don't do that."

He was pulling away, and she wanted him to feel safe enough to share with her. "I'm not. I just want to understand. You don't have to hide anything from me."

"It's not easy, so don't expect miracles. This scar, it's nothing. It wasn't even one of the bad days."

She leaned into him, cuddling up in the crook of his arm. No more words. The strong sound of his heart soothed her. The fact he'd opened up at all said a lot. He was trying—for her. Right now, she just wanted him to feel safe sharing, to know she wouldn't judge him.

It wasn't until later that night when Brick left with a lot of the boys when someone knocked on her door. Her nerves were already on edge. She hated being without Brick, but mostly she worried if he'd get hurt—or worse.

"Hey." It was Ally, Lord's old lady. They'd chatted a few times but hadn't spent too much alone time with each other.

"Hi."

"Could I come in for a few minutes?"

Callie shrugged and stepped aside. "Sure." She'd been warned to behave herself with Ally because she was at the top of the pecking order with the women. Lord wouldn't tolerate anyone being rude to his woman.

Ally sat on the armchair next to the bed. There wasn't much room for company in their bedroom. For some reason, the vibe Ally gave off calmed Callie somewhat.

"When I first came here, it wasn't under ideal circumstances, trust me. It wasn't even willingly. Everyone hated me. The other women even beat me up pretty bad in the beginning until Lord dealt with them." She ran a hand through her hair. "What I'm trying to say is that I understand what it feels like to be the new girl. I know some of the club pussy can be a real pain in the ass, but you learn to ignore those ones. If they push you too far, you come to me."

She smiled. It was nice to know someone else had her back. The entire MC lifestyle was so new to her. "Thank you."

"I'm serious. It's nice to have you around here. And I've never seen Brick so happy."

"Really?"

Ally chuckled. "Definitely. Of all the men, I thought he'd be the one to die alone. He tried his best to convince Lord to ditch me, too."

Callie bit her lower lip.

"But now he's different. So focused. I swear you're always on his mind. Lord said he's pussy whipped. But I know the truth."

"What's that?"

"Brick's fallen in love. Our boys, they're not like any other. When they fall, they fall hard. No going back. He'll do anything for you, Callie."

Just the thought of that filled her with a unique satisfaction and maybe a bit of arousal.

"What if they don't come home tonight?"

Ally frowned. "Don't start worrying now or you'll never make it. They're always doing something that's life-threatening, but Lord always comes home. Sometimes I think they're invincible." She laughed.

Callie laughed too. She felt so relaxed, her nerves

fading away.

"Do you have family outside the club?" Callie asked.

Ally shook her head. "This is my family now. My dysfunctional little family. Now you're a part of it." She rubbed her belly. Brick mentioned she was expecting again.

"Are you excited for another baby?"

"Very. Especially Lord. We're kind of making up for our own shitty childhoods, you know. They call it breaking the cycle, but we're just giving our kids the lives we should have had."

Callie imagined having Brick's kids. They'd be beautiful babies. For the first time in a long time, she was looking forward to the future.

THE BIKER'S DIRTY LITTLE SECRET

Chapter Eight

"What's your fucking problem?" Lord asked Brick that night.

"Don't have one."

"Could have fooled me. You look like you've just found out you've got a limp dick."

"Fuck off."

He lifted the binoculars to check the activity outside of Skull Nation. He and the rest of the guys had all done a drive by and confirmed for themselves it was up and running again.

Those fuckers. He didn't know how they did it. Clearly, they had contacts that went a little deeper than the local hardware store.

"I don't like this," Brick said.

"Me neither."

"Something doesn't feel right."

They weren't in any danger, but considering a clubhouse had just been rebuilt, he would have expected a little more celebration going on. There was nothing. He didn't understand it.

There was no joy. No happiness.

Why?

There wasn't even a crowd of guys. Just a couple of bikes in the parking lot and a few of the men wearing the leather cut, marking it as theirs.

"Abort," Lord said.

Brick glanced to the side as he pulled out his cell phone. He dialed each man, giving the alert.

"They know we're out here," Lord said.

He hung up on the last call. "The guys are heading back to the clubhouse. What do you want to do?" he asked.

"I want to stay a while, check it out."

Brick gritted his teeth. Tonight, he was supposed to be taking Callie to the lake, but that was going to have to wait. Work always came first, and he wasn't about to start changing the rules to suit her needs.

You want to be out there with her, fucking prick.

The truth was he wanted to spend as much time with Callie as possible, but now she wanted to know about the past and he had no interest in sharing anything about that. He'd learned long ago nothing good came from looking back. People thought it did, but it didn't.

His life hadn't been a picnic. It had been hard and painful. His mother was an abusive bitch who sought out even more abusive bastards to hurt him.

He'd gotten away, but it had taken him a long time to fight for himself. One of the many reasons he hit first, asked questions later. So long as he got the first punch in, he always came out a winner.

Callie wasn't like that. He got that her past wasn't as clean sailing as he first thought. Her own mother kicking her out of the trailer she was raised in was the first indication, then of course was the way she acted around violence.

Thinking about her mother, he made a note to go and visit the bitch. He was determined to make Callie's life the best it could be.

No one was going to get in the way of that.

"You're just going to be there silent?" Lord asked.

"What do you want me to say?"

"I'm waiting for you to tell me you've got a date."

"Callie can wait."

This made Lord chuckle. "Already fucking up."

"Club business comes first," Brick said.

Lord sighed. "Club business comes first, but you also need to learn to have a life, Brick. To balance it out."

"Why? Because you're a prime example of it."

This made Lord chuckle. "You don't see or hear my woman complaining."

"You spoil her."

"In case you didn't notice, some women are worth spoiling. Don't you want to do the same with your woman?"

"That's beside the point. Callie knows the club will come first." The lake wasn't going to dry up straight away. They had time.

As he thought that, he recalled the memory of her being wrapped around him. The sweet promises he'd made when he left their bedroom. Even now, he didn't think of it as his bed, but theirs.

What was his was now hers, and vice versa. He ran a hand down his face. Now he started to think like a married man. If he went on any longer, he was well and truly fucked.

"I don't know if I feel sorry for you or not," Lord said.

Brick looked at the Skull Nation, trying to figure out what was going on. Their compound was back up and running. There should be many bodies tonight. The destruction would have been easy.

"Do you think they know what happened to Jeff?" Brick asked.

"They know everything, and I bet they're anticipating us to hit back. What I want to know is what they've got planned for retaliation." Lord cracked his neck to the side.

Brick waited.

Lord did this from time to time. Where he spent

moments of silence trying to get into his enemies' heads, attempting to detect their next move.

"If you were him, what would you do?" he asked.

"I'd expect an attack tonight. My guess is the guys who are wearing the leather cuts are prospects or willing volunteers. You don't put your best guys out to be slaughtered. They must be in a safe haven. Somewhere that would make them feel safe, anyway. That's the only explanation for it, but why? If I expected an attack and didn't take the chance to defend, then it's because you have a bigger plan. What would that bigger plan be?" Lord ran a hand through his hair before pulling out his cell phone.

Brick looked over to see him dialing Righteous, the club's chaplain. The one man who probably knew a whole host of sins.

"Anything happen?"

He didn't hear what Righteous had to say.

Lord didn't say anything and then hung up. "I don't like this. We need all the guys to be in church."

"Lord, that's not a good idea. The rat."

He still needed to deal with the lead Copper mentioned.

"Fucking piece of shit. I want to know what the fuck these bastards are up to. It's time to go visit Jeff."

"You want to go to the hospital?"

"It's the only place we're going to be able to go. He'll know something. I just know it, and as for all of this shit, we'll deal with it." Lord looked ready to commit murder. His prez was crazier than him, which said a lot.

They straddled their bikes and took off, riding right to the hospital. They had left Jeff in a bad way. Dumping his ass at the hospital afterward, which was more than he deserved.

THE BIKER'S DIRTY LITTLE SECRET

There was no chance in hell he was going to squeal.

Brick felt the wind across his face, but rather than embrace being on the open road, he was ready to explode with anger. He wanted to be back in Callie's arms. The thought of any of the Skull Nation getting close to her filled him with dread. This should have been a done deal tonight. Instead, they were chasing themselves, trying to play catchup.

On arriving at the hospital, Lord made another call to Righteous to make sure all brothers were accounted for. They were. It was just him and Lord now.

They entered the main reception to find an older woman, dark shadows beneath her eyes, looking like she'd enjoyed much better days than sitting behind a hospital reception desk.

"Hey, sweet lady," Lord said.

It never failed to amaze Brick how quickly Lord could turn on the charm.

"How can I help you?"

Seconds ago, the woman looked like she'd been sucking wasps. A few choice words from Lord, and she was ready to be putty in his hand. He wondered if she'd have been so happy to see Lord if she knew he was very happy, married, and in love with Ally.

"We heard that our friend got beat up pretty bad, and well, we only just got the news and we've been riding for a couple of days straight to get to him. No one gave us a room number or a person to contact." Lord reached into his pocket, pulling out some cash as he gave her a name.

Brick waited to see if the woman would accept the bait.

Tick-tock.

She took the money. "Let me see what I can do

for you. He is your brother after all." She gave Lord a wink.

"You are a fine woman."

The receptionist giggled.

He needed to start taking pointers from this guy. They had Jeff's floor and room number. With a final wink, they went to the elevator and stepped on.

"You make me sick," Brick said. "You're one of the scariest motherfuckers around and look how you worked that woman."

"It's a gift. One day, you'll have the same kind of gift, just not as good," Lord said.

"Is that why you and Ally never argue?" Brick asked.

"Ally and I don't argue because I know how to treat a woman good. You need to start shutting up and taking notes. A wealth of knowledge here." Lord tapped his head.

"You're down nearly two hundred dollars for this information," Brick said.

"But without my charming personality, we wouldn't be here at all, would we?"

They stepped off the elevator and went to find Jeff's door number.

Lord leaned against the door with a sigh. "We know what we want?"

"All the info on the Skull Nation. Easily done."

A nod from Lord, and then they entered Jeff's room. He was watching television. He dropped the remote, his hand shaking as soon as he saw them.

"I didn't do anything. I didn't say a word. I swear. I swear." The machines he was hooked up to started to beep.

Brick smiled. "We're not going to do anything." Lord sat down in the chair nearest the bed. "We have a few questions." He reached into his jacket pocket and placed the muzzle of the gun against Jeff's knee. "This is either going to be easy or hard. I know what I want, and I know what is good for you. Tell me, Jeff, are you going to be a good boy?"

Jeff was already perspiring.

"I think Jeff pissed himself," Brick said.

"I know, so I guess I'm not that scary. We all know it's way more fun when they shit themselves."

"No, please, please, please," Jeff said, putting his hand near his leg as if to ward off any threat of being shot.

"Then how about you be a good boy, and you tell me everything I need to know about my good Skull Nation brothers."

****

Brick never came home.

Callie waited until close to midnight before getting changed into some night clothes. Losing her virginity had been a big deal, and Brick hadn't even cared enough to come home. The following morning, he still hadn't come home. There was no sign of him. She went down to the kitchen, and like so many other times before, was ignored by the rest of the club. They only paid her attention when Brick was around.

The way they were with her made her wonder if he did this regularly with women. Brought them to the club, slept with them, and then did the vanishing act.

She took her breakfast of a couple of slices of toast outside. It wasn't a warm day, and she wrapped the cardigan around her to try to ward off the chill.

She wished Ally would pop by again to give her some words of wisdom. Being in a relationship with a biker was like walking on eggshells. Maybe Brick just wasn't relationship material like Lord was for Ally.

There was no point to it. Nothing had changed. She and Brick were the same as before.

Was he sending her a message she hadn't read clearly enough? He wanted her gone?

Callie's appetite faded fast.

Without another word to any of the club, she made her way into the clubhouse, past the main room, and up the corridor stairs, going straight to his room. There, she grabbed the bag off the floor, placed it on the bed, and reached for her things. She refused to stay with a man who didn't want her.

The idea of going to the lake on a date with Brick had meant something to her. They didn't know everything about each other but enough to move onto the next step, and she was more than ready to do that, but clearly, Brick was happy to not have a future together. She'd given her virginity to a man who only wanted to use her.

Tears filled her eyes. Was that what he wanted? To use her?

Just the thought of it made her feel the fool. No, more than a fool, a stupid, blind idiot. The first guy to come into her life and show her some nice attention, and she'd fallen for his act.

That was exactly what it was … an act. He didn't care about her. He lied to her. There was no love here.

"What's going on here?" Brick asked.

Callie jerked up. She had been so upset and distracted by her own sadness she hadn't heard Brick enter. Glancing at the bed, she squared her shoulders. "Nothing. I'm going to head back to my place. I think it's better this way."

"Better? Callie, babe, you're not going anywhere."

"I have to go." She ran fingers through her hair.

THE BIKER'S DIRTY LITTLE SECRET

Her hands trembled, and she hated that he saw her like this—teary-eyed, struggling, close to losing it. Brick had made her feel so much, and slowly, he'd torn her apart.

Brick slammed the door closed.

She held her ground, refusing to move as he came toward her. "I don't know what game you're playing, but I don't want any part of it. I'm not ... this isn't who I am."

He stood right in front of her, grabbing her bag, and she watched as he tipped out the contents so they landed on the floor. "Let me get one thing straight, Callie. You're not going anywhere. What part of me telling you that I loved you didn't you get?"

"All of it. You lied."

Brick frowned. "When the fuck did I lie?"

"You lie about everything. You lie all the time. Isn't this what you do? Find women, sleep with them, and then get rid of them?" she asked.

"Wait one second, I never said anything like that. Has one of the guys said anything?" he asked.

"No. I just ... I know ... okay. I get it."

"For fuck's sake, I don't do that. First of all, I don't have to. Open your eyes and you'd see there's a lot of willing pussy around wanting me. Second, I have never in all of my years told another woman that I loved them. I never even told my mom, Callie. You are the woman I'm in love with. I had club business to attend to last night." He cupped her face, tilting her head back.

"Club business?"

"Yes. It ran on longer than it needed to." He pressed his head against hers. "I'm not going to lie to you. The truth is ... I didn't want to have this conversation with you, talking about our pasts, so I put off going to the lake."

"Oh," Callie said. Guilt filled her. "You didn't

have to do this. We don't have to talk about anything you don't want to." She touched his hands where they held her. "I'm sorry."

"Don't be sorry."

She felt ever so guilty. He slammed his lips down on her, and this time, she cupped his face. His tongue traced across her bottom lip, and she released a moan as he pulled her close to him. The hardness of his body was such a turn-on.

Brick let go of her face to run his hands down her back, going to her ass, drawing her close, and deepening the kiss as he plundered her mouth. He broke the kiss to trail his lips to her neck, biting down before sucking on the flesh beneath her ear.

She arched up, feeling an answering pull between her legs. She didn't want him to stop. His name was a moan spilling from her lips.

"I don't want you to ever leave me, Callie." The hands on her ass moved up to cup her tits.

"I won't leave you. This was a mistake."

He smiled. "Are you sore?"

"No. I need you."

"I don't want to hurt you."

"You won't. I know you, Brick. I want you. Please. I'm not as soft as you think. I can take you." She wanted to feel him deep inside her, fucking her, claiming her, making her forget everything.

Brick moved her back toward the bed, and she went willingly.

He dropped her down and she tugged at his leather cut. Then he stepped back, removing his leather cut and letting it drop to the floor before grabbing his shirt and tugging it over his head.

She ran her hands over his chest, loving the tight muscles and the ink that covered him. In her haste this

THE BIKER'S DIRTY LITTLE SECRET

morning, she'd only put on a pair of sweatpants and a large shirt. He stripped them off her within seconds.

Releasing a chuckle that quickly turned to a moan, he placed his hand directly between her spread thighs. "This pussy is all mine."

"Yours," she said.

"Good." He grabbed her knees, spreading them open, and then his tongue glided between her slit. The single touch made her arch up and gasp. She never wanted him to stop as he teased her pussy. "So fucking tasty. I want to spend hours eating this pretty cunt."

"Please," she said.

"Do you want to come?"

"Yes. Yes, Brick."

"Then be a good girl and come for me. I want to swallow you, and then you'll get my dick."

He flicked her clit, holding her ass still as he ravished her pussy. She was so close, and when she came, Brick didn't stop. He continued to taste her, licking and sucking at her cunt until he sent her hurtling into a second orgasm.

Her body was no longer her own.

The pleasure filled her veins as he moved between her thighs. He placed the tip of his cock against her core, but slid through her slit, bumping her clit as he did.

Brick repeated this action a couple of times, making her gasp and moan for more.

"Yeah, fuck, baby, that's it. I can't wait anymore. I've got to have you." He put the tip of his cock at her entrance and slowly slid inside her. At first, there was a bit of pain, not like before. This was different. With each inch he plunged inside her, the fuller and needier she became. "I love how wet you get for me."

She grabbed his waist, watching as his cock filled

her until with a long hard thrust, he was deep inside her.

He took hold of her hands, pressing them above her head and locking their fingers together.

"Who do you belong to?" he asked.

"You."

"You're going to get my name inked on your body, and you're never going to have any doubt that you're mine."

Before she could say anything, he slammed his lips down on hers, and she melted. Brick wasn't taking no for an answer, and part of her liked that. She wasn't afraid of him. For once in her life, she finally felt loved. Some women might not want to be with a man like Brick, she wasn't one of them.

All of her life, she'd been pushed aside, unloved, unwanted, but with Brick, he made her feel cherished, and the truth was, she saw a future with him. The real question was if he saw a future with her.

THE BIKER'S DIRTY LITTLE SECRET

Chapter Nine

"I found something. You said you wanted me to come to you before going to Lord."

Brick already had a headache from all the shit going down lately, but this could be a ray of hope. "Go on," he told Copper.

"I built a signal detector. Something I noticed when I tried it out this morning is that it goes on and off when the boys ride out."

So, it was an inside rat. Brick still hoped it was something simple like a hacked cell phone, but when was anything easy for the club?

"We've got a lot of riders. Have you been able to narrow it down?"

He nodded.

Brick scrubbed a hand down his face. "Give it to me."

"I've got it narrowed down to seven."

He exhaled. "Give me the list. I'll deal with it."

All his focus needed to be on the Skull Nation drama unfolding, but now he had to add a possible rat to the mix. He'd thought Lord had exaggerated. The prez was always paranoid. But the threat was real.

He made his way to Lord's office. They got some good intel from Jeff yesterday, but it was only so useful when someone in their own club was selling secrets to the Skull Nation. It was fucking dangerous.

The door was partway open. Lord had Ally sitting on his desk as he stood between her legs. They were kissing and didn't hear him knock. He knocked louder, clearing his throat for good measure.

"Come in, Brick."

Lord smacked Ally on the ass as she scampered

out.

He waited until she was gone before entering, then closed the door behind him.

"I'm guessing this is serious." Lord rounded the desk and sat in his oversized chair.

Brick slapped the list of names on the desk in front of the prez.

"What the fuck is this?"

"One of those is your rat," Brick said.

Lord sat straighter and checked out the seven names. He shook his head. "Not possible."

"Best-case scenario, they've got a bug on their phone."

"That has to be it. These are some of my best fucking men," said Lord. He appeared visibly distraught, leaning back in his chair, both arms behind his head. As he stared off into space, Brick stood on the sidelines and waited for direction.

He checked his watch.

"Get them all in my office. Now."

Brick didn't say a word. Lord was fucking pissed off. He left the clubhouse and whistled for the nearest prospect, telling him to round up the seven brothers.

His mind was fractured, thinking of a future with Callie while wondering what the Skull Nation was up to this time. If they didn't have some semblance of peace, she wouldn't be safe. He also had to open up to her if he wanted to keep her, and that wasn't an easy task. Brick had big plans for Callie. She wasn't a whore he planned to dump once he had his fill. She was the real deal, and he planned to make her his old lady one day. First, he wanted to get that girl registered in college, make her dreams come true. She deserved it all, including a man better than him—only he wasn't optional.

All the men but two were present. As they all

THE BIKER'S DIRTY LITTLE SECRET

filed into Lord's office, Brick was on his cell phone, calling in Tank and Whisky. He couldn't help that his mind went right to the gutter. They weren't at the club, so what the fuck were they up to? Whisky had only been living at the clubhouse for about a year, so Brick still wasn't sure of his loyalties even though he'd been patched in years ago. He'd been living up north, watching over some of their other properties. Tank, well, that would be a stab to the heart if that motherfucker betrayed the Straight to Hell MC. That bastard had saved their asses too many times to count.

"Cell phones on the desk," Lord said. He didn't leave it open to discussion. His tone was eerily calm.

Copper stepped forward with whatever contraption he'd put together and scanned their phones. Brick held his breath, hoping this was an easy fix.

"All clear," Copper said.

"Where are the other two?" Lord asked.

"On their way home, boss." Brick tucked his phone into his pocket.

"You know why you're in here?"

Most of the men shook their heads.

"A rat."

An invisible chill passed through the room—even Brick felt it. They'd all witnessed Lord torture and kill his own men if they were unfaithful. News of a rat in the mix was no joke.

Tarmac put up both hands at the elbow. "I swear to God, Lord—"

"Don't," Lord interrupted. "I don't want to hear it. Until I find out who it is, this club isn't secure."

"Get out," said Brick.

Once they were alone again, he began to pace.

"You think it's Whisky, don't you?" Lord asked.

He shrugged. "No. Yes. I don't fucking know."

"I'm not going to crucify a man based on a hunch."

Brick glared at Lord. "I'm an animal now? I just trust Tank over Whisky."

"Don't trust anyone."

"When they get home, I'll have them sent in here immediately. No time to hide their shit. I'll get Copper to scan them straight away before they know what's up."

"You called them home. If one of them's guilty, they're already suspicious," Lord said.

"Whatever. This ends today. We have enough on our plates without having to deal with this bullshit."

Lord opened a drawer and pulled up a 9mm. He checked the clip. "If Tank's the one, you going to put a bullet in his head?"

They held eye contact. "I'll do what I have to do."

Did Lord think he'd gone soft because he loved Callie? Did love equal weakness in Lord's eyes? He wouldn't think twice about doing his job as VP.

"Ally's pregnant."

"Again?"

They had a new baby and they were already having another.

Lord chuckled. "I like her pregnant. And I like being a father even more."

"It doesn't worry you? I mean, kids in this mess?"

"We'll get everything handled. Don't forget, there will always be drama, always a rival knocking at our doors. What matters is loyalty. That's what keeps us safe. If we have each other's backs, no one can stop us."

He nodded. "You're right."

The distant echo of motorcycles captured his attention. He headed out to the yard to round up the last

THE BIKER'S DIRTY LITTLE SECRET

two potential rats. Nobody was off the hook just yet.

Brick watched as Tank rolled in, parking in the yard. The man was a brick shithouse, the biggest guy in the club. He was treasurer and kept track of their finances. By the time he walked in his direction, Whisky rode through the gates.

"Were you together?"

"Together with who?" Tank asked.

"Never mind. Where were you?"

"I was tracking down the lead you got from Jeff. I've been dealing with shit all day."

"And?"

"I know where they're holing up."

Once Whisky was heading their way, he led them back to Lord's office. He stood to the side as the boys entered and faced off with the prez.

"Phones on the desk." Lord scratched his temple with the barrel of his gun.

Copper immediately scanned the phones.

Nothing.

Lord set his gun down hard on the table. "Fuck."

The room got too damn quiet—until Copper spoke up. "Lord."

The prez looked up.

"The sensor went off a few minutes ago. The guy you want recently rode in."

Brick and Lord made eye contact.

"The phones are clean. Check their bodies," Lord said.

Copper scanned both men, but they were clean.

"What's this about?" asked Tank.

This time, Lord stood up, both hands on the desk. "We're searching for a fucking club rat, and I'm looking at him right now. Odds say it's one of you two."

"Fuck no!" Tank shouted.

"Don't look at me," Whisky said.

Lord glanced at Copper. The resident tech wiz was inked to the nine. A reclusive but deadly motherfucker. "The bikes."

"Right. Let's head outside, boys."

The bright light of the afternoon sun glistened off the chrome. Before Copper even finished scanning, his sensor was going off. He got down on his back, reaching up under the fender. When he sat back up, he had a small device in his hand.

He'd taken it off Tank's bike.

Even though Tank was bigger than Lord, the prez grabbed him by the shirt and practically dragged him back to his office. He shoved him inside, and Tank barely kept his footing.

Brick slammed the door shut, leaving just the three of them.

"I trusted you," Lord said. He turned and punched him in the jaw, a spray of blood coating his white t-shirt. He shook out his fist.

"I'm not a rat." Tank held out a hand. "I know what this has to be about."

"Then let's hear it before I get really angry."

"I went out last night looking for the Skull Nation hideout. There was this slut at the gas station, so I took her to a hotel for the night. I fucked her three times and she left first thing in the morning."

"I don't need to hear about who you fuck," Lord said. "You keep that shit to yourself."

Tank scrubbed a hand down his face. "When I looked out the window, I saw her get on the back of a Skull Nation bike. There were three of them, so I didn't want to act alone."

"So you were targeted?"

"I can't say for sure, but if there was a tracker on

THE BIKER'S DIRTY LITTLE SECRET

my bike, I'm thinking yes."

Lord paced. "You're a fucking idiot."

"I know. I know."

"You have plenty of pussy around here, for fuck's sake." Lord ran a hand through his hair. Brick could tell the tension was easing.

"You didn't think to tell me?"

"I followed them at a distance. They wanted the upper hand, but I found out where they're staying."

Brick put two and two together. "If the bitch put the tracker on him today, then we still have a rat. Someone gave Skull Nation information when you first brought Ally here. It's more than a tracker and going on longer than one day."

Lord ordered them both out.

He knew something had upset his prez, but he did as asked and left his office. They'd definitely be paying the Skull Nation a visit soon.

****

"Why the rush?" Callie asked.

"I don't have a lot of time. If I know him at all, Lord will call a meeting tonight."

She didn't even want to know. Life in a motorcycle club was constant chaos, but somehow, they always handled things. Even though she'd been around for a while now, she still appreciated all the little things, from having all she could eat to not smelling piss in the stairwells. She expected the worst, but this place was worlds better than where she'd come from. Most of all, she felt safe with Brick. Loved. This was where she belonged, and just imagining going back to her old life gave her chills.

She wrapped her arms around his waist as they drove off on his Harley. His abs were hard and ripped with muscle, so she couldn't help but slip her hands under his shirt as they drove. His skin felt warm.

Callie rested her head against Brick's back, so in love with him. She just needed to get used to him coming and going at odd hours and heading off on dangerous rides every now and then. He said he was loyal to her, so she needed to trust him. It was a challenge to keep her jealousy and nerves at bay, but she was trying her best.

They slowed down near the small town. She used to walk there from work when she didn't have cab money. It was only a blip on the map but the only place she ever frequented. They passed the restaurant Brick had taken her to on their first date. He was replacing all her bad memories with new, happy ones.

He entered the mall and parked his bike. Once he cut the engine, she immediately asked why they were there.

"There must be a list a mile long you keep telling me about. This is your chance to get everything you need. There's a good chance we'll be on lockdown soon, so I want you comfortable."

She didn't ask any questions because she didn't want to hear the answers. Instead, she just took the offer at face value. What could be wrong with shopping?

"I don't like spending your money, Brick."

"You're mine. Don't think that way. Besides, I'm the one who didn't let you go back to work, so blame me."

It was odd not needing to work anymore. She used to sell her soul for a paycheck.

They entered the market where they had a grocery store in back and fresh farm produce in the front. She usually couldn't afford any of the good stuff, but Brick took a cart and told her to add whatever she wanted. When he grabbed a can of whip cream and winked, her body immediately reacted. The man was

THE BIKER'S DIRTY LITTLE SECRET

sinfully delicious and knew how to tease her.

"I'm buying this too, so don't complain," he said.

Brick put the chocolate cake in the cart. It looked delicious. She wanted to shout at him for tempting her when she was trying to watch her weight but bit her tongue. Life was too short to not enjoy simple pleasures, especially when her boyfriend loved her curves.

Then she saw him. Her body immediately recoiled, a wave of nausea threatening to make her sick. Her uncle was in an aisle, looking at the canned food. He tucked something into his jacket. She hadn't realized she'd been standing frozen in place when Brick jostled her.

"Baby, what's the matter?"

She forced herself to focus on him. "Nothing."

"You look like you've seen a ghost."

Callie shook her head. "Let's go." She tugged him in the other direction. The last thing she needed was for her uncle to spot her. Most of her relatives were criminals, addicts, or both. It was embarrassing. Plus, she didn't want a confrontation. This uncle, in particular, was abrasive and rude, and he'd definitely say something to upset Brick.

Her heart calmed a degree as she put distance between them and her uncle—until she turned around and realized Brick wasn't there.

She abandoned their cart and rushed back to the canned goods aisle. Brick was nowhere in sight, but she caught her uncle's attention as she rushed over.

"Little Callie Johnson, is that you?"

All she could do was breathe. Her feet felt like lead, and her mouth wouldn't work.

"Your mother was wondering where you'd gone off to. She said you owe her. The fridge broke within a week after she moved into the trailer. Fuck, she was pissed with you."

She opened her mouth to argue, but no words came out. Her family brought out all her insecurities. Once again, she was a little girl in the midst of the dysfunction.

Then he was there. His strong hand on her side, his breath against her ear. "Aren't you going to introduce us?"

"Ain't he a little old for you?" Her uncle looked Brick up and down in the same judgmental way she was well familiar with. "Or is he just a sugar daddy? You don't look like you've been suffering."

"You should mind your business." Brick took an aggressive step forward. She didn't want him to get hurt. He had no clue her family was dangerous. They had no value for human life or decency.

"Who the fuck are you?" he asked.

"I'm the man taking care of her."

Her uncle laughed. "She sleeping with you for rent money now?"

Brick shoved him, a couple of cans falling from inside his jacket. Her uncle reached in his pocket and flipped open a knife, brandishing it back and forth.

"Uncle Pete, no!"

"Shut up, you little whore. And get this asshole to pay for your mother's fridge. Otherwise, you won't be happy when she finds you."

She should be used to this, but it always cut deep.

Brick reached out faster than her eyes could follow, snatching the knife and twisting her uncle's arms until he begged for mercy. He whispered in her uncle's ear. "I'm going to burn that fucking trailer to the ground. And I don't give a shit who's inside, so tell her mother not to sleep too lightly." He twisted his arm further, making him cry out. "And if you see Callie around, do me a favor and pretend you don't know her. She's nothing like you, and never will be. If I find out you so much as speak to her and move your junkie ass within ten feet of her, I'll come and find you. I'll take my time before I put a bullet in your brain. Do you understand? Nod if you understand."

Her uncle Pete nodded rapidly. Brick shoved him away, then took her hand, leading them back to the cart.

"What was that about?"

"No one talks down to you. No one, Callie. Don't fucking forget it."

She looked back over her shoulder. "He's been to jail."

Brick chuckled. "He's a petty criminal. He's a joke and waste of our time."

Callie couldn't argue with him. It felt so good to watch Brick put him in his place and put some fear in him when he'd terrorized her for most of her childhood. She felt liberated.

She held on to Brick's arm as they continued shopping.

After they paid for their supplies, they walked out into the parking lot. Callie pointed at a guy smoking in front of the diner. "That's one of them. One of the Skull Nation guys who used to go to the lumber yard."

Brick looked over, but the asshole already had his sights on them. He scoffed as he loaded the supplies into the compartment on the back of his bike, not taking his eyes off the enemy. Just then, his cell phone dinged. It was a message from Lord. He wanted everyone in church.

Chapter Ten

Brick stared around the church meeting as Copper did the preliminary scan of the room. All the guys were present. The club was supposed to be dealing with the Skull Nation problem, but so far all they'd been focused on was the rat.

He looked at all the brothers, waiting to see which one broke into a sweat and gave the game away.

No matter who it was, it would be a huge disappointment. No, it would break his fucking heart when he found the person who'd turned their backs on them.

Just the thought of one of their own going to the enemy with club secrets turned his fucking stomach. He believed he could trust everyone in this room, but that was total bullshit. There was no trust here.

Once Copper showed them the guilty bastard, that would be it.

He tapped his fingers against his leg, feeling the anger simmering beneath the surface.

Copper growled. "It's no one here. Can I … I want to scan shit around the room. Can I?"

Brick looked toward Lord, who seemed ready to explode. The boss nodded.

"Go ahead. I'm not leaving this room, and I'm not going on the road until our rat is located."

Lord pressed his lips together as Copper started to go around the room, scanning inanimate objects.

The shit in the clubhouse had never been an afterthought. There were pictures of naked women, football memorabilia, car posters, and junk from tradeshows. He'd never added anything himself. Copper moved around the room, and then he stopped, clicked his fingers, and pointed at a picture frame of a limited-edition bike.

Lord tensed up.

Brick remembered him laughing as he brought it into the room not long after he'd started to get serious with Ally. Much to their surprise, Lord had taken Ally on the road, and they'd stopped at a garage sale or a market, he couldn't remember where.

Ally had used the last bit of money she had to buy this for Lord.

Lord had never been given a gift by a woman. It had a huge significance for the two of them. It cemented the couple's bond.

"Are you the rat?" Brick asked.

Lord shot him a glare.

He expected him to smash the picture, to drag Ally back into the room to demand answers, but as he turned the picture over, opened up the metal clips, and removed the back, there it was, a singular listening device planted behind the picture.

Copper took it out, threw it to the floor, and stomped on it. Bits of metal scattered.

When he pointed his device at it, there was no more signal.

"It would seem I have to apologize," Lord said. His hands clenched into fists as they rested on the table.

"You need to bring Ally in here," Righteous said.

"No, I fucking don't. Ally isn't a traitor. She's my woman."

Brick watched him put the picture frame back together. Anyone looking at Lord who didn't know him would see a carefully controlled man.

He knew differently.

Lord was angry. More than that, his rage knew no bounds, and seeing as they used his woman, and a peaceful moment between them, he wanted to make them hurt. Now that was something Brick could live with.

"I want to go scan your bedroom," Copper said.

"What?"

"You heard me. For peace of mind for the club, for you. One of us could have died based on that listening device."

"If you boys think this stops me from ruling, then take me on," Lord said. "Request me to fight for my leadership."

Brick looked at the boys.

"It's not about your ability to rule," Tarmac said. "When it comes to Ally, you don't see straight."

"You want me to get rid of my woman? The mother of my child?" Lord asked.

The whole room went silent.

Brick didn't want Lord to give up his old lady. With Ally around, life got a whole lot easier. There was a time Lord was impossible to be around. He was a big fucking bastard who was known for his moods, and to be honest, Brick liked settled-down, relaxed, daddy Lord. He was a lot nicer to deal with on a daily basis.

"I won't ever give up my woman," Lord said. He started to remove his leather cut.

"No," Brick said, standing up. "You're not getting rid of Ally. I get it. They don't. Put your cut back on." He turned toward the group. "None of you get a say about any of this shit." He grabbed the picture frame. "This could have happened to anyone. Just be thankful Copper found it before it was too late. There was no rat to begin with, which explains why the Skull Nation didn't react to everything we did. Not all of our business is dealt with in this room. They got lucky with this, but no more. You got a problem with Lord, you take it up with me, but I'm not voting our best fucking club president out because his woman bought a dodgy picture." He pointed at each of the brothers in turn. "All of you have brought something into this room at some point. It could have happened to any one of you. It just so happened to have been Ally, and we all know that woman is so fucking unlucky. Look at who she ended up with."

Lord shook his head.

"You want to vote him out, then you vote me out," Brick said.

He loved the club, but he wasn't willing to stay with the club if they couldn't overlook a simple, innocent mistake like a listening device. Their enemies sought out every opportunity to get the upper hand. They'd be more careful from now on.

Staring around the room, he waited. Righteous leaned forward, elbows on the table.

"Are you going to give us the plan to get rid of those fuckers? Because I, for one, need a drink."

Brick started to laugh. Righteous was their chaplain, but he could drink anyone under the table.

For the next hour, Lord gave them all the information and the plan of attack for taking out the Skull Nation hideout.

Once it was all done, the brothers left one by one, leaving him alone with Lord. He held the picture in his hands like it was a treasure.

"You okay?" Brick asked.

"Yeah. You do know this is dangerous, don't you? That there's a chance we won't make it out alive. Real death shit."

"I get that, but I also know those guys are sloppy. They're not going to be able to get the jump on us. They never could before. They're not going to do it now. Just another day, Lord." Brick slapped him on the shoulder and turned toward the door, only to stop and look back at his club president. "Would you leave?"

Lord looked up. "I'd fight for my place here, Brick. You know that. The club is my life, but I can't give up Ally and my kid. They complete me. Everything else, it doesn't compare. I'm sure you feel that way about Callie."

"I can't let her go," he said. "I think about it all the time. A good man would let her go and let her find someone who deserves her. I'm not that guy. I can't handle the thought of her being with anyone who isn't me."

"Then don't. But you make sure you're the one in control of her happiness. You're the one responsible for a good life or a bad one. I know Ally deserved a better life and I vowed never to hurt her. I aim to make her life the best it has ever been." He held up the picture frame. "If I was to tell her about this, she'd be heartbroken. Ally hasn't got a malicious bone in her body. She would never do anything to harm me or this club. We're her family."

"Will you tell her?" Brick asked.

What was discussed in church would stay in that room.

"No," Lord said. "What I will do from now on is every time she gives me a gift, it will be scanned. We'll keep Copper busy."

"Does she give you gifts all the time?" Brick thought about Callie. She'd given him one of the best gifts of all, herself.

"All the time. I love her so fucking much." Lord glared at him. "Don't think for a second I'm turning into a fucking pussy. I'm sharing this shit with you because you can relate."

Brick laughed, holding up his hands. "I know what you mean. I thought pussy was just for the fun of it.

THE BIKER'S DIRTY LITTLE SECRET

You wet your dick and you move on. Don't get a clinger, and you stay the fuck out of trouble." He shrugged. "I never knew it could be like this."

"Who would have thought it, eh, you and me, in love with two women who really don't fit into this club."

"Who the fuck does?" Brick asked.

****

Callie sat on the edge of the bed, a nervous energy taking control of her thoughts. She'd been here since Brick had gone into church, unable to focus on anything else. Ally had wanted to sit and chat, but she couldn't do it. Her nerves were shot. She knew Brick was going to be organizing the take-down of the Skull Nation, and it terrified her. She'd seen those men firsthand when working at the lumber yard. They weren't going to play games.

She loved Brick so much.

She'd never felt this way about anyone before. Callie had always kept to herself, never allowing herself to open up to others. When her own family would throw her under the bus for the simplest thing, trust didn't come easy.

What if something were to happen to Brick? She pressed her palms together and sent up a silent prayer to whoever was listening in the hope they'd hear and be able to help Brick through this time.

The door opened, and she jerked out of her thoughts. She didn't expect to find Brick smiling.

Getting to her feet, she threw herself at him. In the back of her mind, she knew she shouldn't be acting like this. There was no reason for it, but she couldn't help it. He hadn't gone to deal with club business yet, and it was so good to see him.

Brick wrapped his arms around her. His hands went straight to her ass and she let out a gasp as he gave her a squeeze. "Now this kind of welcome I could get used to."

"I don't want you to go," she said.

"Babe, you know I've got to go. There's no stopping me." He pulled back and cupped her cheek. "You don't need to stress out about it."

"The thought of anything happening to you…"

"Hey!" She wanted to talk, but knew he was only going to stop her anyway. "Stop. Nothing is going to happen to me. Do you know why?"

"You're Brick?"

"No, because I've got the entire club at my back and a woman I need to come home to."

Tears filled her eyes. "I'm that woman?"

He laughed. "Who else would it be? Who else has made me pretend to be a chicken farmer?"

She started to laugh with some happy tears, then his lips were on hers, and she didn't care what he said or what he did, she only wanted to feel his affection.

With the way Brick's hands roamed up and down her body, she felt on fire with need, hungry for more, desperate to feel his touch.

Within a matter of minutes, he had her stripped completely naked. Her clothes were strewn on the floor, and Callie took care of his, admittedly with a lot less finesse. She wasn't used to removing men's clothing and it showed, but with each hard muscle revealed, she became more aroused.

Brick kissed her hard on the mouth, hungry, as he backed her up toward the bed. With each step they took, her need heightened to a fever pitch. She couldn't stop it. He broke the kiss, trailing his lips down her body, going to her tits. He sucked on each nipple in turn before gliding down toward her pussy. A trail of heat followed the path of his lips, her body on fire.

THE BIKER'S DIRTY LITTLE SECRET

When he touched her pussy, she felt like she was going to come completely apart. The recent tension, the fear, her love—it all morphed together into a desire that needed fulfilling. He stroked his fingers between her thighs, running from the entrance of her pussy up to her clit. Brick knew exactly how to touch her, making her writhe with need. He circled her bud, pressing down, then slid back inside her.

She whimpered as he moved so his lips were right above her pussy. This time, she went to her elbows and watched as he slid his tongue through her slit, sucking her clit into his mouth.

Closing her eyes, she threw her head back, moaning his name, not wanting him to stop as he ravished her body.

"I want you to come all over my face, Callie. Let me have it."

His tongue was like magic as it danced across her skin. Each stroke, each touch, sending her heightened senses into overdrive. She couldn't stop it. Only bask in the pleasure and never let it go.

Brick started to build her orgasm, but he changed paths, moving down to fuck inside her with his tongue. She rocked against his face, not wanting him to stop, needing to come.

He moved up, taking her clit once again. He used his teeth, soothing out the pain with his tongue and stroking up and across. His fingers plunging inside her, stretching her. He was everywhere, and she loved it.

Her orgasm was so close, hanging on a precipice.

Just a few strokes of his tongue, and she came apart, screaming his name and begging for more, and he gave it to her. On and on, the waves of her orgasm left her spineless on the bed.

Brick didn't stop straight away, allowing her

orgasm to ride all the way out, drawing every last drop of pleasure from the moment. He kissed up her body, going to each of her tits and flicking his tongue against them before going to her mouth.

She tasted herself on his lips, but she didn't care.

The tip of his cock ran up and down her slit, nudging her, making her moan for more. With each touch, she couldn't contain her need, and she let it out in a guttural groan.

"That's it, fuck, baby. I've got to be inside you. I need to fuck you, feel you wrapped around my dick." He slammed his cock hard and deep within her, making them both moan from the rush of pleasure.

She wrapped her legs around his waist, thrusting up to meet him for each slam of his cock. Brick took her hands, pressing them above her head and holding her in place as he rocked inside her. At first, his movements were slow, sure, controlled, but she saw the fire within his gaze.

Her man was holding on by a thin thread.

Callie gyrated her hips, and it was like she flicked a switch as he pumped inside her, going deeper and harder, taking her to heights only he could bring her to.

She didn't think it could get any better, but then he pulled out and spun her around so she was on her knees. His actions were so swift she didn't have time to complain as he ran his fingers all over her ass, spreading the cheeks—then his fingers were inside her.

"You have such a pretty ass," he said.

She whimpered. What more could she do as he pulled those fingers from her pussy and drew them back to tease the puckered hole of her ass?

"Shh," he cooed. "Don't tense up. There's no reason to tense up like that. I've got you. I'm going to make this so good."

THE BIKER'S DIRTY LITTLE SECRET

The press of his finger was strange but not ... uncomfortable. He pushed his finger and there was a slight sting, nothing too bad. And oddly erotic.

She gasped.

"Yeah, you're going to be so tight here. Tell me I can, Callie. Tell me I can fuck this ass and fill you with my cum."

How could she deny her man anything? He was her entire life now.

"Yes," she said.

She wanted to be everything to Brick, but she also trusted him to make this as good as it could be. Callie wanted to be able to give him anything those club whores were capable of.

Brick worked a single finger inside her, in and out, getting her used to the feel of him. Then he added a second finger, and with this, he began to stretch her out. She nibbled on her lip, eyes closed, trying to focus on just how good it felt rather than anything else. Every time he wiggled his fingers inside her, he hit something that drove her need higher. She wanted this, her curiosity piqued.

He was ... wow, she couldn't think or focus. It was so good. He took his time, even adding a third finger, and this time, there was a small amount of pain, but as he stroked her clit with his other hand, any residual discomfort vanished. She was more focused on her needs.

"You're ready," he said.

She didn't tense up as he released her body and then he moved behind her. He nudged her down so she was flat on the bed, with a couple of pillows beneath her stomach to lift her just enough for him.

"I'm not going to lie to you, Callie, this might hurt, but if it's too much, tell me. I *will* stop. Got me?"

"Yeah," she said.

He pushed his cock inside her pussy. "I want to get it nice and wet. I would've used some lube if I had some, but I'm all out."

His words shouldn't sound dirty to her, but they did, and as he pressed the tip of his cock against her ass, she tensed up.

"Trust me."

She took a deep breath as he began to ease his cock within her ass.

"Push out."

She frowned but did as he asked, and then his cock began to fill her, inch by thick inch.

It was too much. She held her hand up and he stopped immediately.

"I don't…" She ended on a moan as he began to play with her body, working her, and she felt the instant hit of pleasure as it rushed through her body.

This time, she pressed back, taking more of his cock within her as he stroked her clit.

"Fuck me," Brick said.

"No, fuck me," she said. "Fill my ass with your cock."

They both groaned as he sank the last of the way inside her.

It was tight, a little uncomfortable, and really fucking weird, but it was Brick. He was her man, and she wanted him so badly.

"You drive me fucking crazy, Callie. You're mine. I ain't ever letting you go."

She was never going to go anywhere.

She loved Brick. He was the man she wanted to be with for the rest of her life. Even if he was a biker and did illegal things, he treated her like a queen. Her grandmother once said that it wasn't what the man did

THE BIKER'S DIRTY LITTLE SECRET

that was the problem, it was the way he treated those around him that counted. Brick was loyal. He was a man far more deserving than some who never went on the wrong side of the tracks.

Brick began to thrust in and out of her. At first, she didn't like it. Him inside her ass, it was way too strange, but then slowly, she felt that fire burning inside her. The way he touched her, bringing her to life, and the feel of his cock was just too good to deny.

He worked her pussy, and she felt the start of her second orgasm. He didn't stop, bringing her to the edge of release. As she came, she felt him move a little faster, going deeper inside her, and then the hard pulse of his release as he filled her.

His growl echoed in the room. His arms surrounded her, wrapping her in the warmth of his embrace, and she knew without a shadow of a doubt, there was nowhere else she wanted to go.

Chapter Eleven

"Where?"

Tank ducked down and pointed through the trees. Brick could see the faint flicker of light intermittently in the distance.

He stood straight. "Fucking pussies. Hiding out like animals." Brick turned and faced the group of men shrouded in the darkness. "We go in fast and hot. Anyone in that hideout is game. No questions asked."

Lord groaned.

"Second thoughts?" Brick asked.

"We need at least one of them to interrogate. I want to know how they rebuilt without a prez or VP. We killed all their top brass, but they've been busy spying on us and expanding."

"You hear that? We need answers from at least one of those fuckers."

It was time. Brick was more than ready. Their revenge was a long time coming. Tank and Rancher had sustained serious injuries after their last shootout.

After the Straight to Hell MC took out all their top men, they should have focused on finishing the job rather than hoping they'd disband.

Now, ready to face off again with the Skull Nation, something new stirred inside Brick. Normally, he ran in with no fear, no hesitation. If he died, he died. Now he had something to live for, a woman to go home to at night. It made a difference.

He had to use caution now. Callie still suffered from her grandmother's death. Little things like the smell of fresh apple pie made her tear up. Even driving by the old trailer made her emotional. He didn't want someone telling her he'd died, too. She'd have no one. He had to

THE BIKER'S DIRTY LITTLE SECRET

consider more than just himself now.

They all mounted their idling bikes and hit the gas. No one expected them. Now that their clubhouse was clean of any listening devices, they had the element of surprise.

Brick was out front with Lord and Tarmac. He steered with one hand while getting comfortable with his semi-automatic in the other. It would soon be raining lead. The scent of gasoline, pine, and adrenaline was potent. Light grew stronger as they neared on the narrow path. They were practically on top of them now.

A door burst open, the shadow of a big guy in the backdrop of light stood there with a rifle. Within seconds, he was down. The Straight to Hell MC scattered around the series of small cottages in the woods, revving their engines, shooting everything that walked.

One of their men went down, and Brick wasn't even sure who it was yet. It enraged him, and he went on the hunt, emptying clip after clip into his enemies. This wasn't a democracy, it was survival of the fittest.

A bullet whizzed by his head, bringing his focus to the three men in front of him. They converged on his bike and it dropped to the side. He shot one point-blank in the throat, blood spraying out like a fountain. The other two didn't have guns on them. He pivoted out of the path of a fist before using his own. Two of them were on him, pounding and punching, trying to rip off his cut. It only fueled his rage. He pulled out his blade, using a mix of fighting skills, brawling, punching, and cutting when he had a chance.

He stabbed one of them straight in the heart as the last bastard grabbed him from behind. The following gunshot rang his ears, the shrill echo stealing his hearing. It was Righteous, the motherfucker shot the guy behind him in the head. He was on the ground. Righteous was the one who'd been shot.

It was pure chaos, loud and dark. Brick tried to keep focused, but even in the midst of battle, Callie crept into his thoughts. They didn't leave any spot untouched during their search. There was no mercy tonight, only blood and revenge. The barrage of gunfire started to ease. He put up his hand, signaling the men in his view to back down. Brick listened as his hearing slowly returned.

Quiet.

"Please. No." The squealing pleads grew louder. Brick couldn't see anything until Stump held the Skull Nation prospect into the headlights of several bikes.

Stump shoved him forward and Lord appeared from the darkness like an apparition.

"No prez. No VP. Who's in charge now?"

Whoever it was had to be pushing daisies after tonight. They'd taken out every biker in this makeshift hideaway.

"I don't know anything."

Lord grabbed him by the scruff of the shirt with one hand and backhanded him with the other. Their prez wasn't gentle. The man was a beast and didn't do mercy.

"Please…"

"Name," Lord said. He pulled a handgun from his waistband, pressing it against the biker's thigh.

"Okay. Okay."

"I'm waiting. Don't test my patience."

"Steel. It was all Steel."

"What's his rank?"

"He was patched, moving up the ranks. Once everyone was killed, he took over, rallied the troops, and led our rebuild. He knew where the prez kept the money."

"Why you hiding out here?"

"Steel said it was part of the plan."

THE BIKER'S DIRTY LITTLE SECRET

Lord shot him in the leg, and he dropped down to one knee, letting out sounds that were a mix of whimpering and laughing.

"Now that your new leader is dead, I'm hoping that's the end of this. You fuckers are like cockroaches."

Their prez held the muzzle of his gun to the man's temple. The biker only chuckled. "Oh, he's alive and well. The Skull Nation will live on no matter what you do to me."

Brick stepped forward. "Where is he? At your new compound?"

The prick smiled and shrugged. "You'll kill me anyway. I know your game."

"End the fucker," Brick said, walking away. He wouldn't talk anymore. It was in his eyes. The acceptance of his fate. Once a man knew there was no hope, they were dangerous.

Lord pulled the trigger, the body slumping to the ground. Their victory felt tainted. The new leader of this Skull Nation revival was still out there, plotting and planning. Or was this prospect just blowing smoke up their asses? There was no way to know right now.

He walked over to Righteous and reached out a hand, helping him to his feet.

"Where you hit?"

"Right shoulder and leg, I think," Righteous said.

Brick pulled the other man's bike up and tested it out to see if it was functional, doing a couple of circles. "You okay to ride, or do you wanna ride behind me like a bitch?"

Righteous just raised a brow.

At least they'd sent a message loud and clear, Brick was alive, and soon he'd be returning to his woman.

The next day, he slept in until past noon, which

wasn't the norm for him. Even before he opened his eyes, he felt the softness of Callie's body cuddling up next to his. She'd been asleep when he returned late last night. He hated to wake her but knew she'd be worrying. Brick had slipped into bed next to her after showering. She'd whispered she loved him before falling back to sleep. It was only then that Brick realized she'd been the first person to claim to love him.

Today, he was going to start making things right for Callie. He'd erased her old life, so he owed her a new one. A better one.

When he finally opened his eyes, Callie was staring at him. "You're sleepy today," she said.

"Long night. Way too long."

"Is it all over now?" she asked.

He didn't have the heart to tell her the truth. Brick nodded.

"We can't stay in bed all day. Get dressed, baby. I have to do something with you in town today," he said. "And don't ask. It's a surprise."

She scowled but did as he said, taking a quick shower and dressing. Today she wore a floral sundress, and she looked fucking adorable. That lush body of hers was his in every way now.

"We're going on my bike. You going to straddle me with that little dress on?"

Callie shrugged. The thought of her pussy pressed against him from behind already made him hard. He pushed the ideas out of his head so he could stay focused on his task.

They headed downstairs and mounted his bike. She wrapped her arms around him before they rode off toward town. After his surprise, he wanted to take her to the river like he'd promised a while ago. He was still debating if he'd actually go through with it or not.

THE BIKER'S DIRTY LITTLE SECRET

Oversharing made his skin crawl, but he wanted to show Callie she meant more to him than sex. She was his everything. His joy. His strength.

He parked on the public lot shared by a government building, library, and local college.

"What are we doing here? Is everything okay, Brick?"

"Come on."

He took her by the hand and led her up the wide concrete steps. As they walked up, he leaned over and whispered in her ear. "I'm registering you in college."

****

Callie kept turning back to make sure Brick was there. She was in line to register—for college. This was all too surreal because it was a dream she never expected to see come to fruition. She wished her grandmother was still alive to tell her, to make her proud.

She took a deep breath. Breaking apart now wasn't a good idea. Without Brick, she wasn't sure she'd ever have been able to go through with this. The time, money, and knowhow were things she didn't have. Brick said she could apply as a mature student. He'd done all the legwork before bringing her here.

The college was bustling because it was registration week. It took a couple of hours to get everything completed, but she was officially enrolled in their business program. Maybe she could help out the club. She wanted to pull her own weight and not only rely on Brick and the Straight to Hell MC for everything.

When she was waiting for her student card to be laminated, a guy shifted closer to her.

"What program?"

She smiled. "Business."

He nodded, looking her not so discreetly up and down. "What's your name?"

"Callie."

"Cute. How'd you like me to show you around campus?"

"Sorry, I don't think my boyfriend would like that," she said. Why would she be interested in a pretty college boy when she had a real man, hard and deadly?

"You have a boyfriend?"

By his tone, she could tell he thought it was a brush-off. Before she could ensure him by turning around to point at Brick patiently waiting in the lobby, he was there. He must have seen the other man getting too close and personal.

She felt the heat of his body behind her.

The guy took one step back. "Hi, I'm Brian."

"Fuck off." Brick's hand came possessively around her stomach, holding her tight to his body. When the college boy rushed off down the hall, he leaned down and kissed behind her ear.

"I wonder if he thought you were my father," she teased.

She supposed it wasn't out of the realm of possibility, considering the age gap between them. "Watch your mouth, baby girl. Or mine won't be between your legs tonight."

Callie almost melted to the ground, her thoughts in the gutter. Brick was so good with his tongue. She twisted in his arms, resting her palms on his chest. His hands encircled her loosely around the hips. "Thank you."

"For what?"

"Everything. Caring. My own parents wouldn't have done this for me. It means more than you could ever know."

"You're smart, Callie. You're going to go far. I won't be the one to hold you back."

THE BIKER'S DIRTY LITTLE SECRET

"Does that mean you want me to spread my wings once I have my diploma?"

He gripped the back of her neck, forcing her to look at him. She let out a little yelp as he was less than gentle. Her pussy tingled. "I'll give you the world, Callie, but you'll always be mine."

"Yes," she whimpered. "I'm yours."

"Callie Johnson." Her name rang out, pulling them from their reverie. She turned to the counter and took her identity card, staring at it for longer than she should. This was really happening.

When she looked up, Brick was staring at her.

"I'm proud of you, baby."

"I haven't even done anything yet."

"You will." He took her hand. "There's one more place I need to take you to."

"Another surprise?"

"You could say that."

They got back on Brick's bike. She felt all the eyes on them, and it made her proud to have a sexy biker as her boyfriend. She doubted anyone would mess with her now that she had Brick. No more being everyone's punching bag. No more being teased because she was overweight.

She rested her head against Brick's back as they rode back in the direction of the clubhouse. The wind through her hair, vibration of the engine, and her man between her legs was an addiction. She never thought she'd ever feel comfortable on the back of a bike, but she loved riding with him.

They started to slow before getting home, so she looked around. Brick steered off the main road, the path getting bumpier and branches brushing her arms. He stopped the bike near the bottom by a river shrouded by mature trees, several of them weeping willows. It had a fairy-tale feel.

"Is this the place you told me about?" she asked.

He got off the bike and helped her to her feet. Without answering her, he turned and kissed her hard, desperately, while reaching up her dress. She felt his passion, his intense need to claim her. Callie closed her eyes and tossed her head back as he trailed kisses down her neck. He pulled her panties to one side and impaled two fingers deep into her cunt. She sat down heavily, taking more, her breathing already labored.

"Aren't we supposed to talk?" She could barely say those few words.

"Do you really need to know what broke me to know that I love you?"

"You love me?"

"Besides the club, you're all I have. All I want," Brick said.

He was right. There was no point in rehashing a tragic childhood just to feel understood. She'd been through hell and back in her short life, so she knew what made him tick. For him to admit he loved her meant a lot. It was all she needed to hear.

"You're my man." She reached out and cupped his erection with her hand, squeezing just hard enough to make him groan.

"Don't think I love you any less because I don't say all the flowery words. I'm committed to you. Only you. I consider you my old lady."

"Am I?"

She knew the significance of what he was saying. The club pussy talked about old ladies like they were royalty or something. No one dared to mess with them. They were the chosen few. She saw the way Lord adored Ally. Callie wondered if Brick would ever officially claim her as his.

THE BIKER'S DIRTY LITTLE SECRET

"I'll make the announcement during our next meeting. Everyone will know exactly how I feel about you." He ran a hand over her hair and looked at her with pure adoration. Brick made her feel like a princess. "Tell me a secret. Something you shouldn't have done or something you should have told me."

She tilted her head, wondering where he was going with this. "I haven't done anything wrong, Brick. You're the only man I've ever been with."

He shook his head. "I'm not accusing you. I'm not mad. I just want you to go first. I can't stand to see you upset with me."

Callie wondered what he'd done that he felt he had to confess. She knew he loved her but wanted to clear the air before making her his old lady. Hearing that he'd been with another woman when she loved him more than life itself would shatter her to pieces. Now she had to go first, confess something to Brick.

She thought for a bit.

"Most of my family are addicts. They steal to support their habit. I swore I'd never become like them, never date a man with a criminal record."

"Good thing I don't have one." He winked.

"That's not it," she said. "I know what you are and it ... turns me on."

He raised a brow. "You like having a bad boy. Such a naughty girl." Brick backed her up until he had her pinned against a large tree. "How about I fuck you right here, right now? Hard, just how you like it."

"Not yet. I want to know what's eating away at your conscience first."

He exhaled, did a little spin with his hands in his hair. "I don't want you to hate me, Callie. I fucking love you. Sometimes I do things without thinking straight."

"Just spit it out, Brick." Her entire body tensed.

She wondered how she'd respond if it was exactly what she didn't want to hear.

He braced one hand against the tree, looking down. "I burned that fucking trailer to the ground. If you couldn't have it, that bitch certainly didn't deserve it."

She froze. Yes, it was a place filled with happy memories. It was where her grandmother helped raise her later in her childhood. But it had been taken from her. She had no legal rights to it. All she could focus on now was the fact Brick hadn't cheated on her.

"Good."

"Good?"

"When she kicked me out of that trailer, I spiraled downward. I hit rock bottom and had no one in the world to turn to. I wouldn't wish that on anyone." She took another cleansing breath. "I'm glad you burned it down."

He laughed out loud. "I've lost sleep over this, woman."

"Now you know, don't keep secrets. They're bad for your health."

"Except you, you're my dirty little secret." He hoisted her up against the tree, the rough bark scraping her ass. She wrapped her legs around him as he fiddled with his belt. "And I'm going to give you this hard dick. It's all yours. You want it?"

"Make me forget my name."

He kissed her with so much passion—love, anger, desperation. They were one and the same. And she hoped nothing ever came between them.

Chapter Twelve

"You do realize you look like a giant pussy," Lord said.

"Fuck off." Brick hooked his fingers against the tie that seemed to be digging right against his neck. Why did people wear these fucking things? He wouldn't ever understand.

"Do you have any doubts, man?" Righteous asked.

"None."

The boys were pissing him off by constantly questioning his decision. It was one he was going to stick to because unlike a lot of the guys in the club, he knew when he had a good thing.

"Where's Ally?" he asked.

"You know where she is."

Helping to convince Callie to get changed into the expensive wedding dress he'd purchased. Brick hadn't gone for the traditional proposal like a normal person, no, not him. He decided to plan the whole thing by himself, with a little help from Ally. Actually, to do this in top secret had required a lot of work. Ally had organized the decoration of the clubhouse, and much to his annoyance, it looked like a pink explosion. It was ... girly. No one would have thought for a single second this place housed scary-ass bikers. It was a joke. He hoped no one outside the club ever heard the truth.

Brick had acquired a tux, a wedding dress, and a priest. That was all he needed. When he told Ally his idea, she'd laughed at him and asked him if he was joking. Not exactly the best thing for a guy who intended to marry the love of his life to hear. So instead of doing what he thought was best, he gave Ally full rein.

Staring around him, he wondered if that was a mistake. The wedding cake was in full view, five tiers, with little dolls on the top that reminded him of something from a voodoo horror movie. The brothers were having the time of their lives, but at Ally's insistence, they were all wearing tuxes. She wouldn't accept any of them dressed in leather, not even her man.

At least she knew how to keep them in line. Flowers were everywhere as well. Anyone with allergies was up shit creek.

"I can't believe you're ready for this, man," Lord said. "I never thought I'd see the day a pussy got you wrapped around her little finger."

Brick laughed. "We both know Callie's not like any other woman. Same as Ally's not like any other. They're special."

"They're ours. It's what makes them special."

It had been over a month since they took out the remaining Skull Nation club. At least, the ones they knew about. Steel was still gone—if he even existed. Brick honestly didn't know, but he went with his gut which suggested he was out there.

Someone pulled strings in the background.

Whoever Steel was, he was clever. He nearly tore their club apart with worries of a damn rat, and all this time it had only been a damn bug.

He dreaded to think of what would have happened if Copper hadn't discovered it. The club would have been in some dire straits. No one would have trusted anyone. Now, as a precaution, a general sweep of the clubhouse was required. Lord was keeping Copper busy.

Each time there was a scan, Brick was always tense. He trusted his brothers but knew deep down at any point, a traitor could be lurking. Steel had managed to instill doubt, and Brick was doing everything he could to ignore it.

"Any news?" he asked.

Brick needed to distract himself from the nerves. With Callie not knowing he intended to marry her, and spending the last couple of weeks keeping his distance, he worried what she might think.

"None. There's no guarantee Steel even existed, but I've got sources checking it out. If they rear their fucking heads, we'll take them out."

There was no doubt about it, Lord was on a warpath to take out the Skull Nation. He couldn't blame him. If those bastards were alive, there was going to be trouble.

The guys all mingled, glancing over at him, waiting.

Brick checked the time for the umpteenth time. "Have you heard from Ally?"

Lord pulled out his cell phone and shook his head. "No news is good news."

"Or Callie's skipped town because she realizes what an asshole I am."

"Wow, you sound scared."

"Wouldn't you be?" Brick asked. "If this was Ally?"

Lord chuckled. "I wouldn't have given my woman any chance to doubt me."

"Bastard."

Brick's hands clenched and released. He took a deep breath, trying not to panic. Callie was the love of his life, and this had to be the single most romantic thing he'd ever done. He'd been thinking about her the entire time.

At night, his thoughts were on her. He spent hours watching her sleep, holding her in his arms, breathing in her scent. It was hard to believe this woman had picked him out of every other man in the world.

He knew how fucking lucky he was and wouldn't waste a moment of the gift he'd been given. With the life he led, he didn't deserve an angel—but one had fallen into his lap.

"Give me your damn cell phone," he said.

Lord snorted but didn't fight him as he took the cell phone and dialed Ally's number. He happened to notice the number of times Lord called her. The couple was rarely apart, but it clearly showed the prez was obsessed with his woman, too.

"Hey, baby, not much longer."

"It's me, Brick."

"Hey," Ally said.

"What's the holdup?" he asked. "Is she there?"

"She, er, she doesn't understand why I want her to try on the dress. In the end, I told her that a friend really wanted to see it, and I needed her to wear it. Callie's not very trusting, is she?"

Brick laughed. "She a little freaked?"

"I think I've gone from her favorite person to her least favorite one. I don't know how I'm going to get her downstairs."

The brothers had worked long into the night to get the clubhouse looking like this. Ally had organized everything, stored it all in the warehouse around back, and then he'd taken Callie upstairs and spent the entire night fucking her into oblivion so she wouldn't wander downstairs.

He and Ally had switched places in the morning, and now it was up to Ally to get the bride to her own wedding.

"The hormones," he said. "Act like a crazy woman. Do whatever it takes to get her down here."

THE BIKER'S DIRTY LITTLE SECRET

"Damn it. I'm not good at lying."

"Please, Ally, I'll owe you one." He hung up the cell phone before Ally could scare him with any of her demands.

Lord, in response, chuckled. "I've got a baby with another on the way. Are you sure you just did the right thing?"

"It can't be that bad."

"Have you met me?" Lord asked. "They're my spawn, Brick. Damn, you must be desperate because she'll have you babysitting, no doubt."

This wasn't going exactly how he hoped.

Brick glanced at the priest, who looked at him in pity.

Not good.

Time kept on ticking by.

He heard a text message coming from Ally. "They're on their way down."

"Okay, here we go." He moved through the brothers and Lord rounded them up to get into position. Silence fell on the room once they settled into place.

Brick moved toward the door that led up to the bedrooms. Running fingers through his hair, he stopped. Then, the door opened.

"He's going to go crazy when he sees you," Ally said, her voice loud and clear in the hush. She was talking a mile a minute as she pulled Callie into the main room, and Brick fell in love all over again.

Ally had shown him six dresses. He'd hated all but this one. Tight to the body, highlighting every single curve of her luscious figure. The fullness of her tits and hips, the small waist. The only downfall to the dress was it went down to the floor, hiding her thick, juicy thighs that were designed to be wrapped around his waist as he fucked her hard and fast.

"Brick?" she asked.

"Callie." He was mesmerized. Lost in thought. She was even more beautiful than he remembered.

"What's going on?"

He had no idea. He couldn't look away, nor did he want to. Ally patted his shoulder. "This is the part where you go down one knee."

"Oh, yeah, right." He slid down and reached into his back pocket. "Callie, I'm in love with you. Have been since I walked in as a chicken farmer. I love you more than anything else in this world. I want to marry you. To make you happy, to put my kids inside you."

"Be careful, there's a priest," Lord whispered.

Righteous had wanted to perform the ceremony, but he wasn't fit to stand up. It had pissed him off because he'd asked Brick to wait, but he couldn't be patient. He had to put his ring on her finger as soon as possible. Waiting around wasn't an option for him.

"Ask her to marry you," Ally said.

He glared at her.

"Marry me, Callie. Please, and make me the happiest man on earth."

He stared at her, waiting. Hoping, his nerves firing hot.

"You did all of this for me?" Callie asked.

Had he been presumptuous? What if she didn't want to marry him at all?

"Yes. I need you, Callie. I didn't want to wait."

"Which is the only reason I'm not up there," Righteous said, interfering. "I wasn't getting healed fast enough for the big guy."

Callie laughed.

"Is that a yes?"

She cupped his cheeks and laughed. "Of course, it's a yes. It's a big fat yes." She slammed her lips down on his, kissing him hard. "I love you, and yes, I will marry you. I want to spend the rest of my life with you."

Wrapping his arms around her, he stood and pulled her close. It was the best answer he could have hoped for.

****

One week later

Callie stared down at her wedding band. When Ally had trapped her in her room, she had no idea what the hell was going on or what Brick had planned. She'd brought in a dress and some crazy explanation about her trying it on. Callie usually humored her friend, but everything felt off.

At first, she'd declined. Ally had gotten emotional, and Callie had panicked since she was expecting another baby. But it had all worked out in the end.

After the priest had declared them man and wife, and Brick kissed her, he'd told her everything. How he'd originally intended to have their wedding. She was really pleased Ally had stepped in. Brick's plan had sounded cute, but it wasn't the kind of wedding she would've wanted.

She'd only get married once, and well, this was her first and only.

Much to her surprise, Lord had presented them both with a honeymoon package. They'd been taken away on an all-expenses-paid trip to a luxury island that offered sun, sand, sea, and relaxation. The resort was peaceful, quiet.

When they arrived, she had seen loads of people, but since being shown to their private villa, with their own view, she hadn't even heard anyone else.

Brick had loved it.

So had Callie when he showed her exactly how

good it was to be all alone. It had been her first time on a plane, her first vacation ever. They were able to connect on a new level.

The ocean was hard for her to go into as she had this fear of sharks and giant sea creatures. Brick had distracted her by making love to her.

He'd told her the island offered tours and other amenities, but she was happy to be left alone with only Brick for company.

He told her things might be a little stressful when they got home. Callie had been even more surprised when he'd told her exactly why they would be.

"I don't want to keep you from club business," he said. "Some of the guys don't share shit with their women, and that's fine. With you, I don't want any secrets between us."

"Oh," she said.

He'd told her everything. About Steel, the Skull Nation, the listening device. He didn't leave anything out. Brick had asked her if she remembered someone called Steel from the lumber yard, and she hadn't. At work, she'd been made to stay well clear of the biker club.

She gladly stayed away from them.

Sitting on the sand on an oversized beach towel, the sun beaming down at her, her thoughts were on the Skull Nation. From the moment they walked into the shop, she knew they were bad news, but hadn't said anything. At the time, she needed the work, and years of learning to look the other way with how she grew up, she had done so as well.

"Hey, baby," Brick said, coming out and handing her a cocktail.

She removed her glasses as she looked at him. "Hey."

THE BIKER'S DIRTY LITTLE SECRET

He pressed a thumb to her forehead. "What's got you frowning?"

She was a little distracted by his nakedness. Brick refused to wear any clothes, so his full muscular body, covered in ink, was on display. He looked droolworthy. She was glad there were no other women around for her to be jealous of. No one else would look at her man.

"Skull Nation."

"Don't let it bother you, babe. Believe me, we've got it more than handled."

"But I think there is a way I can help you."

"Not happening. You're not being used as bait or any of that shit."

She rolled her eyes. "I'm not talking about bait. I'm talking about the shop. I know I didn't handle them, but Jeff did. He had to have started a paper trail, right?"

"Not if they paid cash for everything."

She frowned. "No, we would have still had to do an invoice or something. There was too much stuff moving."

Brick took a sip of his cocktail. She couldn't help but laugh as it had a little umbrella perched on the edge, with lots of cherries in it.

"Are you mocking me?" he asked.

"The image, it doesn't quite add up."

He wrapped his arms around her, pulling her close. She cried out as some of her drink spilled down her body.

"Look what you did," she said.

"Look what I did." His tongue traced the path that her drink had taken. Her eyes closed, and her mind went straight to where his tongue traced down. She felt the cold spill of liquid close to her bikini bottoms.

She touched his face. "No, no, I have to finish what I'm saying." She had to stay on track before he directed her thoughts to far more pleasurable things. "When we get back. I can go into the office."

"Not happening. I don't want you near that asshole. You no longer have a job there anyway, remember?"

"I was a good worker. I heard Jeff was struggling to keep staff."

"How did you hear that?"

"When I was grocery shopping, one of the women in line was talking about him being a horrible man to work for, and that she'd quit after a single day. He's mean, it's no lie. I stuck around because I needed the job."

"And if you think I'm going to put you in that position again, you're fucking mistaken."

She pressed her lips to his, silencing him. Once she had him distracted, she broke the kiss. Their cocktails were long forgotten, being soaked up by the sand where they'd fallen. "I know you wouldn't do anything to hurt me, and it's one of the many reasons I love you."

"Good of you to remember."

"I'm part of your club now," she said. "I couldn't bear for anything to happen to you. I don't even want to think about it."

"Then don't."

"Then let me do this."

"Callie."

"Brick, if I can get that job back, I can find the paperwork."

"Assuming he hasn't burned it."

"He still has to run a business, and for tax reasons, he has to keep the paperwork for a length of time. Trust me. I can make this work." She wanted to help the club. They were her family, her friends. Once she had her college diploma, she'd be even more of an

THE BIKER'S DIRTY LITTLE SECRET

asset.

Brick pressed his head against her chest. His tongue danced between the valley of her tits, and she couldn't help but chuckle from his onslaught. "You're not playing fair."

"I don't want you to ever be hurt. I know what that fucker is capable of, and if he does anything…"

"Two weeks. That's all I'll need. Two weeks when we get back. A week for him to watch me like a hawk and for him to build up trust again. The next week for me to take over, and to, you know, find everything."

He stared at her.

She waited.

"You know it's a good idea," she said.

"It is, but I don't like it."

"Do you not like it because I thought of it or because you're worried about me?"

He grabbed her hip and tugged her beneath him. "The second one, babe. You know what you mean to me." His lips played across her neck, and she gasped as he sucked on the point at her neck that sent waves of pleasure rushing through her entire body. "I swore to love and protect you."

"You will."

"You don't have to do anything for the club."

"I'm doing it for you," she said. "All for you."

He slammed his lips down on hers. Brick devoured her. "I love you so fucking much."

"Do we have a deal?" she asked.

"I still have to run it by Lord, but otherwise, we have a deal. I'm going to be staying close, and that fucker will be six feet under if he ever puts his hands on you, do you understand me?"

She cupped his face, kissing him passionately. "I understand. Now, are you going to fuck me and put your baby inside me?"

His eyes flashed fire, and it sent an answering heat through her body. Brick had gotten under her skin since the moment she met him. All she had ever wanted was him, and she knew deep down that was never going to change. It was why she was willing to go find the information they needed.

Her grandma had once said there was going to be someone who she would do anything for, walk through fire or on broken glass for. Callie hadn't believed her. The only men she'd known were the ones she despised and treated her like nothing.

Brick was different.

He treated her like his queen.

She loved him with her whole heart and knew there was nothing that would come between them.

He was her man, just as she was his woman.

They were no longer each other's secret, but now very much out in the open, and in love. The future had always been daunting to her, but no longer. With Brick by her side, and the club at her back, she knew she could do anything.

The End

www.samcrescent.com

www.staceyespino.com

THE BIKER'S DIRTY LITTLE SECRET

EVERNIGHT PUBLISHING ®

www.evernightpublishing.com

Printed in Great Britain
by Amazon